The B⬢⬢B
Girls XII

The Burned Out Old Broads at Table 12

A Novel by Joy Johnson Brown

The Last BOOB Girl Book

ISBN: 978-1-56123-282-6

To order make checks payable to Joy Johnson Brown,
6406 Maple St, Omaha, NE 68104

Phone: 1-866-218-0101

CENTERING CORPORATION
AND
GRIEF DIGEST MAGAZINE
GRIEF RESOURCES

The BOOB Girls: The Burned Out Old Broads at
Table 12 in

The Last BOOB Girl Book

This last BOOB Girl book is dedicated to my two
daughters, BOOB Girls in Training, Jenny and
Janet. Janet has done every set-up and designed
every cover for every book. She is also my
webmaster and keeps my blog on track and my
webpage up to date. Jenny has been an adviser
and co-creator with everything from ideas to the
denim tablecloth at Mary Rose's wedding and at
the launch party.

It's also dedicated to you because there are too
many of you to thank this time. I couldn't stop
thanking with just those of you who helped with
this book, but way back to Phyllis Diller who liked
the book I and gave her words for the covers.

Thank you all for the adventure, the love and your
Grace, Humor, Courage and **Confidence.**

Walking Toward Maggie

From left to right: Marge Aaron with her red cane (Marge Hollingshead), Hadley Joy Morris-Whitfield (Joy Johnson Brown), Mary Rose McGill (Sharon Anderson), Dr. Robinson Leary (Phyllis Mitchell-Butler). Waiting for them, the water-soaked corpse of Maggie Patten, or Maggie's ghost if you prefer, Sue Mouttet.

In the background, Meadow Lakes Retirement Community (Arboretum Village, home of Marge, Ted and Joy.)

"He's dead!"

The three women sitting at table 12 in the Meadow Lakes Retirement Community dining room watched as Mary Rose McGill hurried toward them as fast as she could, dodging between tables, behind chairs, almost pushing seated diners out of the way – hurrying to get to their table.

She stopped, stood beside the empty chair where she usually sat, put her shaking hands on the table and said it again.

"He's dead!"

The three friends looked at her in shocked surprise. Hadley Joy Morris-Whitfield put her hand over her mouth, Robinson Leary put her hand on her chest and Marge Aaron reached out and put her hand on Mary Rose McGill's wrist.

"What happened, Mary Rose?" Marge asked, her voice steady and strong.

"I was watching television and had to go pee," (this was not unusual for Mary Rose) "and when I came out of the bathroom, in just a minute I realized he was dead."

They looked at her.

"Sit down, honey," Marge said, motioning to the chair beside Mary Rose.

Mary Rose sat.

"Now tell us exactly what happened, Mary Rose. Had he been sick? Did he say he didn't feel good?" Marge Aaron, retired homicide detective, had never lost her interrogation skills. Her red cane hung over the back of her chair as if it were listening for Mary Rose to begin speaking.

Mary Rose took a deep breath.

Hadley and Robbie leaned forward to hear her better. Hadley had grown pale.

"I don't know all the details," Mary Rose aid. She picked up one of the cloth napkins from the table and blew her nose. Rather loudly.

"As far as I know, things were just going along as usual then, Wham! He's dead."

The other three looked at each other, Robbie shook her head just a tiny bit.

"This is terrible," Hadley said.

Marge dug her cell phone out of a pocket of her jacket. "I need to call Alphonso," she said softly.

"I can't imagine this happening," Hadley said.

"You know," Mary Rose commented. "He seemed so happy and he fit the part so well."

They looked at her again.

"Fit the part?" Marge asked.

"Of bridegroom-to-be?" Robbie asked.

"Oh, he wasn't going to get married. He changed his mind at the last minute."

They looked at her harder this time. Robbie and Marge raised their eyebrows at the same time.

Hadley's mouth dropped open just a bit. They all three leaned toward Mary Rose.

Mary Rose's nose was red and running. Tears were still brimming over in the eyes looking out from behind the red-rimmed glasses, and her hands were tightly wound together or she would have been wringing them. She wiped her nose on the napkin.

"Dead, dead, dead," she said. "Who will take his place?"

It was becoming a contest to see who could look at Mary Rose the hardest.

"You're looking for a replacement?" Marge asked.

"It will be impossible," Mary Rose sniffled. "He was perfect."

"Perfect?" the three other women said together.

"Perfect," Mary Rose repeated. "He would put on that beautiful vest and be the most handsome, desirable man in the world."

"Beautiful vest?" Marge asked. They all three thought of Wiley Vondra's ancient leather vest that matched his worn and beat-up boots.

"Most handsome?" Robbie added. Her eyebrows raised once more.

"Desirable?" Hadley finished.

"What am I going to do at this time in the afternoons now?" Mary Rose asked.

Once again, they all looked at her.

"What did you both *usually* do at this time in the afternoons?" Marge asked.

Marge had never completed her call to Alphonso Greatwood, the owner of Meadow Lakes Retirement Community. Her phone lay silent on table 12.

Death is no stranger in a community where the youngest person is sixty-plus and the oldest over one hundred years, but Mary Rose's report just didn't sound right.

All but Mary Rose looked at Marge. Mary Rose was looking out the huge floor-to-ceiling windows onto the spacious autumn lawn and quietly shaking her head. Bronze leaves fell silently from the massive trees outside.

What Mary Rose did not notice as she gazed out at the lawn, was a small person in a green suit, black boots with gold buckles and a green top hat leaning against the wall next to the window, trying to hear what she was saying.

"Could it be Geoffrey?" Hadley whispered.

"He doesn't wear a vest. I was sure it had to be Wiley." Robbie whispered back.

Marge shook her head and turned her chair so she could look Mary Rose in the eye.

"Mary Rose, honey, who the hell died?"

Mary Rose unwound her hands and laid them flat on the table. She looked at each of her friends with a sad, sad face and sat down with a soft thud.

 "Wade Wilhelm Wartsoff," she whispered sorrowfully.

"Who?" Hadley and Robbie asked together.

"Wade Wilhelm Wartsoff," Mary Rose answered, somewhat impatiently.

"Wartsoff? Sweet Jesus," Robbie said. She turned her head away from Mary Rose and did a classic eye roll.

"Holy Mother of God," Hadley added.

"Say who?" Marge asked.

Mary Rose looked just a trifle disgusted. "Wade Wilhelm Wartsoff," she said, her nose lifted slightly into the air as if sniffing a bad sausage.

"Just the most famous daytime actor to ever grace the stage."

"Grace the stage?" Hadley asked.

"He was the famous brain surgeon on *As the World Wanders*."

"I hate to ask this," Robbie said, "but what was this surgeon's name on the show?"

Mary Rose gave her a haughty look. "Of course, he was the world-renowned Doctor Dennis Deadlee.

"Oh, of course, a brain surgeon named Deadlee and this time I really mean it – Sweet Jesus!"

They began to laugh.

Mary Rose began to cry.

The small person in the green hat leaned closer against the window. He smoothed the green jacket that matched the green top hat and green pants that came to a tight end mid-calf. He wore light yellow hose. His boots were shining black and reflected the large gold buckles. From a vest beneath his jacket you could see a gold chain with a holder for a large pipe and a bag of tobacco. He leaned closer still and chuckled a soft laugh.

"I really loved him," Mary Rose hickuped. "I watched every day."

"OK," Marge put on her best detective face.

"What killed him?"

"A poisoned scalpel in the operating room. He was pushed by a vicious, homicidal nurse, cut his hand, fell to the floor and died instantly."

"On his back, legs in the air," Hadley added.

"No," Mary Rose said seriously. "Flat on his face."

She looked at them and grinned a slight grin.

"Okay, so it is crazy, but I really, really liked him and this was a big surprise."

"I'll say it again," Robbie said. "Sweet Jesus."

The tiny person in green slipped silently around the corner outside the dining room, his black boots crunching in the fallen leaves blown up against the wall.

Four Girls, Three Guys, And A Dog

Marge Aaron---
"Marge Aaron," she said when she first met the other women seated at table 12. "Marge Aaron. Say it fast and it's..." she paused, smiled, and looked at them. They looked back.

"Margarine!" Robinson Leary squealed after thinking for about four seconds. "So. you'd butter be good!"

Marge was good.

A retired homicide detective brought in to solve the murder of Percolator Rasmussen, a mean old dude who was found dead on the dining room floor, she loved Meadow Lakes. She stayed on as a resident, did most of their driving and every now and then, to keep in shape, solved a murder or beat the crap out of a bad guy.

Table 12's retired homicide detective was an expert at the wheel of the girls' 12-year-old Hummer, never got lost, and knew the Omaha map street by crime-ridden street.

Marge was a large lady who should be a large lady. She would look out of place as a size petite and she enjoyed her body. She was good at "throwing her weight around," and saying, "There's more woman to a big woman." Her hair was a mix of white and gray and her face held many laugh lines. She was strong and healthy.

Except for that one knee.

She had a replacement, but for some reason, it didn't work. She limped. She walked more slowly now. She hurt. She bitched – and rightfully so. Growing old sucks.

To help her along in her walks, she always had in her procession or within reach when she sat, her red cane. The red cane was an accessory all women could use. It had been designed by Marge's brother, who had worked in British intelligence where James Bond was created and housed.

Marge's red cane had bling.

Press one jewel and it turned into a taser. A second jewel was a rifle. A third jewel shot tripping pellets all over the floor. A fourth jewel held a smoke screen and the fifth jewel let knives spring out of the sides. There was a gold lariat in the handle – just like Wonder Woman.

And Marge Aaron was. indeed, a Wonder Woman. Smart. Street Wise. Experienced.

She had been a homeless teenager and now harbored a genuine penchant for social justice. She worried about hurt and traumatized children in our country, demanded fair play for the homeless and wanted a full reform of the criminal justice system.

And this once-homeless Wonder Woman was never without her red cane.

Like the others at table 12, she was a widow. She had been a cop's cop and had married a cop's cop. They had two children and both their son and daughter were in law enforcement...FBI and Police.

Marge had no grandchildren and seldom saw her children. They texted, emailed and talked on the phone or did video chats. They all loved each other and never exchanged a cross word. They were pros together.

Marge believed strongly in independence and freedom – for everyone. Her children having their own successful lives was a fine idea to her.

Marge Aaron was the friend every woman needs. She was big in her heart and in her generosity.

She knew how to listen. She never judged. Friends could lean on Marge – literally – she was strong enough to hold any sorrow and any trouble you might have.

She was the rock.

Big Marge was also involved with a big black man: Alphonso Greatwood.

Alphonso had purchased Meadow Lakes Retirement Community from the evil Busch family of Florida six years ago. Thorny Busch, the older brother, had used his wicked sisters, Rose Busch and Lilac Busch to turn Meadow Lakes into a den of iniquity with gambling, liquor, prostitution and an underground Viagra ring. The Busch's short, wiry and super-tough mother was BeataRhonda Busch.

Alphonso had zoomed in on his scooter because his knees made Marge's look like Lana Turner's on a World War II calendar.

His knees were totally shot thanks to something that made him famous.

Alphonso Greatwood---
had made his move into football when the Dallas Texans pro football team moved to Kansas City in 1963 and become the "Kansas City Chiefs." That same year they picked a young linebacker in the fifth-round draft.

A young, hopeful Alphonso Greatwood sat by the phone, along with his mother, father and two aunts, waiting for the call. Waiting to find out where he would live. Waiting to find out with whom he would play. Waiting to see if he could make it. Even doubting his name would be called.

They waited.

They waited some more.

At last the phone rang. The legendary coach, Hank Stram, himself, called to invite Alphonso to be on his team.

Alphonso Greatwood, huge and young and vulnerable was the most thrilled young man in America that day.

Alphonso would not be a hall-of-famer, but he would be good. He would stay with the Chiefs for years until his knees gave out.

His next career was in sports broadcasting – all on the radio, and he enjoyed it as much as what was then called, "smash-mouth football."

Alphonso was still asked to come onto sports shows, local and national; radio and television, be a commentator, make predictions and answer questions. He reveled in it. He loved it and while he was doing it, he felt one-hundred percent alive and healthy. They even paid him for it.

He got paid a lot in his football days and afterward and he had invested his money well.

He had just simply written a check and paid for Meadow Lakes from his checkbook.

He had never married, but he had enjoyed his share of "groupies."

And today, Alphonso Greatwood, the Great Wood himself, sits in a tremendously over-priced office, in an even more expensive chair, behind a desk big enough to park a small Volkswagen on top. His huge frame was seated so he could see out of the floor-to-ceiling windows that make Meadow Lakes so attractive.

His office was decorated in Kansas City Chief décor and genuine leather.

There is a special niche carved into one corner of the office and that is where the old football idol parks his scooter, the green machine. Alphonso is pretty much scooter bound. When not in his green machine, he uses two canes to get around.

The canes have Chiefs football helmets serving as carved handles. They, like Marge's cane are red, but with black stripes instead of bling.

His knees, so far beyond repair, hurt constantly and when he walks, they somehow make his back ache. It was the growing old sucks syndrome. The green machine, painted green of course, has a passenger seat with, "bitch seat" written on it. Marge has ridden on it now and then, but their combined weight worries the tires. On the oversized and custom-made dashboard are several buttons. Push one button and the theme song of the old television series, "Happy Days," plays. Alphonso chose that because he is *original* Phonz.

The second button blares out the Nebraska Fight Song. Alphonso is a Big Red fan. And in a few days, two hard-working men will arrive and add a third button. This magic button will play the Chief's War Chant. Alphonso loved that. After his football days, whenever he heard it, he stopped and did the tomahawk chop with his right arm.

Alphonso understood how some people thought the name, the chant, the chop, was an insult to the Native Americans. This black man didn't. He wished teams could be named after powerful black leaders, that there could be chants that warned the opposition that trouble was coming, and that all America could have the bravery these names represented.

One day Wiley Vondra stuck his head into Alphonso's office and said, "Hey Phonz. Did you hear the Washington Redskins are changing their name because so many people have complained? They're doing it out of respect for the Native Americans?"

"Say what?" Alphonso said.

"Yeah -they're dropping the 'Washington.'"

It hadn't stopped there.

One day at dinner, Wiley looked at Alphonso.

"Phonz, if you have a Kansas City Chief's linebacker, receiver, tight end and a tackle in a car, who is driving?"

Alphonso just looked at him.

"A cop."

Everyone at their table except Alphonso, laughed and laughed. Diners nearby who overhead it joined in.

And a day later, even Marge, his sweetheart, his one true love had picked it up.

"Hey Phonsie. If you have 53 millionaires gathered around a TV watching the Super Bowl, what do you have?"

Again, Alphonso just looked at her.

"The Kansas City Chiefs!"

Laughter, laughter, laughter.

Even Mary Rose McGill!

"Alphonso. Which position in the Chiefs lineup needs the biggest shoes?"

She smiled her sweet, innocent smile.

"The one that has the player with the biggest feet."

Groan.

Then one day he was going down the hall from his office, using both canes and being as slow as usual, when he met Robinson Leary.

"Hey, Alphonso."

"Hey Robbie."

They passed each other then he heard, "What did the Chief's quarterback say to his receivers? Don't know – it went over their heads."

Groan again.

Then, while watching at DJ's Dugout, their favorite sports bar, all of Alphonso's friends watched his Chiefs stage an impossible comeback and win the friggin' Superbowl.

Ha, ha, ha.

He was sitting at his desk, thinking about all those bad jokes when Hadley Joy Morris-Whitfield stuck her head in the door.

"Alphonso..."

"Hadley, don't you dare tell me a Chief's joke!"

She looked surprised. "I was going to say we're all going to Marks for lunch. Move your fat linebacker ass and come with us."

Hadley Joy Morris-Whitfield---
walked down the long hall with Alphonso, talking about anything but football.

"Crazy Zed Zonker came into the office to complain about a leprechaun running loose on the premises," Alphonso said as he moved his canes forward step by step.

"Zed has the emotional maturity of a puberty-challenged middle schooler and the awareness of an opossum smoking dope, but we love him," Hadley said. "Plus, I don't think leprechauns bound about much off season and it's not anywhere near St. Patrick's Day."

Hadley Joy Morris-Whitfield had more money than God and Warren Buffett combined. Her apartment was only a two-bedroom, but it was beautifully furnished, and she was equally beautifully furnished herself.

She wore tasteful pantsuits, expensive boots and still looked good in just plain tight jeans. Her hair, which had once looked like the old Vidal Sassoon ads, was shorter now and pure white.

She had married well and had liked big men, big dogs and big cars. For that matter, Hadley Joy Morris-Whitfield *still* liked big men, big dogs and big cars.

Her husband had crashed his private plane into a mountain, and she had found herself rattling around in her big house in west Omaha. She had looked at every retirement community in the city and found Meadow Lakes to be most to her liking.

Ten years ago, and in her memories Hadley thought herself to be young then, she had fallen in love with an attractive Indian Sheriff, Wes Longbow, a Native American who insisted on being called, "Indian".

Wes had died six years ago.

Hadley had wondered how many times a heart could break and knew many hearts were more broken than hers. When your heart breaks, for any reason, you are a tiny bird in a storm looking for a safe place to rest.

She remembered a story she cherished. A soldier, wounded so terribly he would suffer the rest of his life, had taken a pottery class for therapy. He had made a vase that reflected the light but had a large, unsightly crack up one side. The instructor offered to fix the crack, but the soldier said, "No – the vase is broken like I am. But that break, that crack, that is where the light shines through."

Hadley had concentrated on letting light shine through her brokenness.

She had succeeded.

Hadley had macular degeneration, the most common cause of blindness in older people and she was definitely an older people. When she had gone to a retinal specialist, Dr. Ed Mcgillicuddy had said, "Hadley, we can help this with a shot in the eye."

"A shot in the eye!?!" Robbie was with her and they said it together.

"A shot in the eye," Ed answered. "Listen, it sounds a lot worse than it is. We give shots all the time and like I said, it sounds worse than it is."

"A shot in the eye!?!" they said together again.

"Yeah, I know. It's a scary thought. We've even had 300-pound football players faint when they've had to have a steroid shot in the eye."

"A shot in the eye!?!" they both said again.

Ed had given her the shot in the eye, and Hadley Joy Morris-Whitfield had taken it like a 300-pound football player.

She fainted.

In the years since, she had had more shots, she stopped fainting and believed firmly and honestly that it was more important to see with the heart than with the eyes.

She had been a professional volunteer and for as long as she could, still took part in the charities she had championed. She loved people and animals and was one hundred percent grateful for her life.

She was especially grateful for her friends at table 12.

She was watching Robinson Leary, because Robbie was the only one in the group who talked about outliving her money and having to move from Meadow Lakes. If that happened, Hadley would insist on finding a way to pay Robbie's rent.

She was sure everyone living at Meadow Lakes had that thought of outliving their resources.

Those thoughts came like shadows in the back of their heads – of something bad happening, of all the money going and having none left. Even Hadley, wealthy as she was, watched the markets. Her son was the vice-president of a stock firm and had her portfolio. She laughed when she told him if she outlived her money it would be his fault.

He laughed, too.

It could happen.

Hadley and Alphonso met the others in the spacious, heated underground garage at Meadow Lakes. When they all went somewhere together, the friends took Alphonso's custom-made van, painted black with, or course, a Kansas City Chief's logo on each side. Wiley Vondra held out his hand to help Robbie onto the running board which Alphonso had designed to lower automatically when the door opened – and to lower only inches above the ground. It did not work as well as he had hoped when curbs were high.

Robinson Leary---
had skin the color of a rich latte. Robbie was almost as tall as Hadley, had hair that was grey/white and cut in the stylish African American short style that hugged her well-shaped head. She was unusually attractive, had gained very little weight as her years piled up, and she walked straight and gracefully. Attractive and graceful, yes; but not drop-dead, strikingly beautiful as her direct ancestor, Marie LaVeau, the voodoo queen of New Orleans.

Dr. Robinson Leary, retired, tenured professor at Creighton University, did not let people know of this family connection. Marie LaVeau; who still had followers, even though she had been dead for years, even though she was thought to be one of the most beautiful women in the world, even though her portraits hung in famous museums; no, Dr. Robinson Leary did not let people know she was a great granddaughter of the voodoo queen.

Robbie thought of those portraits of Marie LaVeau often. She had been forced to look at the most famous one by an aunt determined to have young Robinson know her history. That had been good – kind of. She had stared at the full-length portrait of a fantastically beautiful woman, standing by a table with strange items on it, but what caught Robbie's attention was a one-eyed snake that wrapped itself around her turban-clad great grandmother. The snake's one eye was eye-balling a black chicken and the snake was managing a hungry look. At Marie's feet stood a three-legged dog.

And Robbie had heard the song, with the howling and the guitar.

In New Orleans where the dark trees grow
There's a voodoo queen named Marie LaVeau
She lives in the swamp in a hollow log
With a one-eyed snake and a three-legged dog.

The song would be followed by a long howl from the singer.

Marie certainly had a one-eyed snake and a three-legged dog. She even had a black chicken that wandered into the mix. However, the voodoo queen had not lived in a hollow log, but in one of the most beautiful houses in New Orleans just outside the French Quarter.

Great-grandmother Marie had given Robbie one gift and if she could, Robbie would give it back. Every so often, Robbie would know something was going to happen. Every so often, she would know exactly what it was going to be. Dr. Robinson Leary ignored these visions. She ignored them, but they left her watchful.

Like the time, recently, when the four friends touched a time portal and went back in history when a gun was found at Marks, their favorite restaurant. That morning she had known, without a doubt, that something was going to happen.

It did.

The times she had been with Esmeralda St. Benedict, the gypsy sorceress, it had seemed as if tiny sparks of lightning were present in the room.

Robbie had learned to live with this and seldom mentioned the weird feelings and if she did, she disguised them as intelligent guesses or hunches. It wasn't something to worry about.

Robinson Leary was the go-to researcher, intelligent guru of the group. She often broke into conversations with information no one cared to hear and would never remember.

Her husband had died in his sleep, spooned in her arms in their Old Market apartment. After he died, she had not been able to face the big table near the window that looked out on Howard Street. It served as their office and held their computers, books and current work. The table had always been stacked high with those books, student papers and it always held two coffee cups. She missed him terribly. Even after ten years of friendship with the BOOB Girls and an on-going relationship with one handsome Apache whose hand she was presently holding under the table at

Marks Bistro. A big Apache named

Raven Five Horns---
Raven had become the seventh best friend in the group. He was tall with the high cheekbones and brown skin of an attractive Apache. His hair had streaks of white mixed in with black and he wore it in a long braid down his back. His clothing was almost always black jeans, a black turtleneck and a black leather jacket. His boots were very expensive black leather. He was Indian and he looked the part. Raven Five Horns turned heads when he walked by.

Robbie was the only one of the friends who had been to his ranch, high in the hills of Wyoming. He had played football on teams opposing Alphonso, still had the muscles, and unlike his old partner on the field, Raven had good knees and could still run with a football if he needed to do so.

He, like Hadley's love, Wes Longbow, owned a security company and his consultations brought him now and then to Omaha, or made it convenient to stop in on the way to wherever. This current trip included a long, extended stay. Raven was assigning more and more work to his staff.

What was best – he was on call for Dr. Robinson Leary whenever she wanted him, and he was her protector and confidant. It was a good relationship.

Marge had met Raven's grandfather on their 1898 adventure into historic Omaha and the great Trans-Mississippi Exposition. His grandfather, Raven Three Horns was a young man then, hopeful that the Indians would regain some land and be recognized by their white brothers.

Disappointment, discouragement and death. Treaties were broken, bodies burned, and the Indians herded off into non-livable territories then blamed for their own tragedies.

Raven had cherished his name, took all his five horns and plowed into pro football, worshiping nature and the greats – Jim Thorpe and Jim Brown, whose records on the field still held.

Thorpe was a full-blood Fox Indian and studying his life as intensely as a young boy can study, taught Raven how to study for college and hold a 4-point average even while giving his life to football in the University of Nebraska glory days. Ah – those Devaney years at Nebraska!

He was All American, then All Pro and now he was all Raven.

He kept a watchful eye on the warriors on the field now who had the high cheekbones and the same heritage as he. The first Americans. The ones who were here when Columbus landed. Indians.

Raven knew them all through correspondence and phone calls. There is Sam Bradford, the present Minnesota Vikings quarterback, who is Cherokee. Sam Bradford - a role model among Native Americans. The Jets' Bryce Petty is Chickasaw.

James Winchester, the long snapper for the Kansas City Chiefs, is a full-blooded Choctaw. The Chiefs also have backup quarterback Tyler Bray, who is Potawatomi. Raven continually reminded Alphonso of this fitting combination instead of telling Chief's jokes.

It's better to make a few million on a football field than to stand staring into the sun with leather straps through your chest muscles to beg God to help you reclaim your land from the white man. The sun dance did little to help except add a sad footnote to history.

They were warriors still.

And now, for Native Americans, Thanksgiving is declared a Day of Mourning, for that's when the Indians were first tricked into selling land for diseased blankets that began their death march.

Raven's millions would go to help Robbie if she ran out of money. He liked the idea. He liked Robbie. If Robbie's running out of money happened, he would have to work out a partnership with Hadley. He knew of her determination.

In his old age, Raven was taking up where his grandfather, Raven Three Horns left off. He was becoming a social activist fighting for Indian rights and recognition.

Alphonso helped him when he needed to contact someone in congress, and so did

Wiley Vondra---
who, of all the friends, was the plainest, easiest, and as close to a cowboy as anyone could be.

The girls met Wiley when they first got together at table 12 nearly twelve years ago. They heard rumors about a naked man in the laundry room at Meadow Lakes; a naked man wearing only cowboy boots, a brown leather vest and a Stetson hat – a man who, when he did his laundry, did ALL his laundry.

Midnight.

Laundry room.

Meadow Lakes Retirement Community.

Maggie Patten had thrown open the laundry room door and there he was, brown boots, brown leather vest and Stetson hat, and that was all, sitting behind a card table with a hand of Solitaire and Willie Nelson wailing from a boom box beside him.

A touching domestic scene.

As Maggie pushed the door open, the giant tall case clock in the lobby struck midnight.

Wiley, dressed only in boots, vest and hat or fully clothed, was just a smidge over six feet tall, thin, a little stooped and with a weathered and rugged face.

He had never married or had children. He had been a ranch hand, owned a ranch and loved the broad plains of western Nebraska.

Wiley was a Korean War veteran. He called it, "the forgotten war," and listed it as the first war we didn't win.

War is cruel.

War is destructive in so many ways, and a part of Wiley had been destroyed as well.

He had been on patrol with his platoon. The movie about brothers in battle could have been his movie. They had spread out in the jungle and all at once Wiley came across a young North Korean soldier. Alone. Scared. Certainly, more scared than Wiley.

They had stopped short and stared at each other. *He'll probably be a good soldier when he gets into high school*, Wiley thought, seeing how young the kid was.

The boy started to cry, reached into his pocket and pulled out a photograph. It was a picture of an older, dignified woman and a young, beautiful bride. The North Korean pointed to the picture then to himself. Tears were streaming unashamedly down his face.

Neither of them said anything.

Wiley pointed to the boy, then pointed away from him – ahead of him – pointed the kid into safety. "Run!" he yelled. "Run!"

The boy looked at Wiley, frowned, then headed in the opposite direction, either from fear, confusion or mistrust, thinking Wiley wanted to kill him on the run.

"No!" Wiley yelled.

The kid ran.

The shots rang out.

After a few long minutes, several of his buddies came up behind him. The picture of the bride and mother was sticking out of one man's shirt pocket.

A souvenir.

A War Prize.

"We got one of those damn Kooks," his buddy said.

Wiley nodded.

Now he sometimes cried in the shower.

Now he refused to look at wedding pictures and when they were developed, would only pretend to view those of his and Mary Rose's wedding. Mary Rose knew he cried sometimes.

Had asked.

Had not been told.

The only person with whom Wiley shared his story was in a vision at Fort Robinson when Esmeralda St. Benedict, the gypsy, had taken them there and they had all experienced dreams and visions that let them revisit their histories. He sat with a German prisoner of war and cried and told the German everything, even how he had cried when he hugged his own mother the day he came home. How he kept track of how old he thought the North Korean boy would be now; how the boy would have grown children.

How in some ways when that North Korean boy died, Wiley had lost his own son.

The German hadn't been real, but Wiley's tears and sorrow had been.

The German understood.

It was like the song said, "War! What's it good for? Absolutely nothing!"

So, if Wiley Vondra had not found peace, he had found contentment. He loved Meadow Lakes and the girls. He especially loved Alphonso and Raven. His brothers. Alphonso said they were brothers by a different mother.

Three races.

Three lives together.

What America's supposed to be about.

Wiley's Nemesis at Meadow Lakes was Zed Zonker, a weird old guy who loved to torment Wiley. However, Wiley held a dear memory of Zed being treed by a chicken, and that thought always brought him comfort.

So, with all the ups and downs of life, Wiley Vondra felt he was the luckiest man on earth because his leg was snuggled up under a table at Marks Bistro and it was snuggled up against the leg of the love of his life.

Mary Rose McGill---
who sat beside Wiley, drifting off and thinking
about their wedding.

To think that old people could fall in love!

But love when you're old is just like it was years
ago. Exciting and sweet with a warm, gentle glow.
She remembered the song with those words, a
tender song by Mark Kurtz.

A warm gentle glow.

That's what she felt right now.

They had kidded her and laughed about her
announcing the death of Wade Wilhelm Wartsoff
who played Dr. Dennis Deadlee on television.
Mary Rose had finally seen it as funny as it was;
them thinking it was Wiley or Geoffrey who had
died. When they told Wiley, they thought it was
him, he crashed his head down on the table,
barely missing his bowl of mac and cheese. Marge
laughed so hard she was afraid tears would run
down her leg.

Mary Rose McGill was a retired housewife.

She had stayed at home and raised four girls, all with the first name of Mary. "What can I say? We're Catholic," Mary Rose would tell people. She had been a housewife until she and her young husband had gone to Iowa State University together. Iowa State: the home of Betty Crocker and a huge Home Economics program. She was a "housewife" until Iowa State and the good old boys in academia decided there was too much discontent with women being called, "just a housewife," so they upped the name to "homemaker."

It sounded better and statistics told women how much they were worth monetarily by staying home ad not competing in their man's world. A few women didn't believe it.

Mary Rose became pregnant with their first daughter while she and her husband were sophomores.

Mary Rose never finished college.

She took some part-time jobs where she could take the baby to work with her and became one of the many women working on their PHT's.

That stood for "Putting Hubby Through."

The other babies came soon after her husband graduated, and as they grew into teenage, they began to control Mary Rose's life. It wasn't until she met the BOOB Girls at table 12 that she became her own person.

Mary Rose McGill, because she was loved by three other women who saw her as she could be, became who she could be.

She lost weight.

She threw fourteen housedresses down the garbage chute at Meadow Lakes.

She went shopping for jeans and sandals and pantsuits and slacks.

She, with a little help from Omaha's best hair stylist, dyed her hair blonde.

She got red-rimmed glasses.

She explained in no uncertain terms to her daughters, that she was in charge of her life and to – as the saying used to be – bug off.

Today her husband would have been terrified of her.

But Wiley Vondra wasn't.

After her husband died, her four Marys had pulled a U-Haul into her driveway, loaded it with some of her furniture, and moved her to Meadow Lakes without even asking if she wanted to go.

Last Christmas their only gift from their mother was a thank you letter.

She loved Meadow Lakes.

She loved her friends.

She especially loved Wiley.

Mary Rose McGill was the one who, every chance she had would say:
Older women are beautiful!
Just look at us.
Our faces are sculpted and chiseled by joy and sorrow, tears and laughter.
Our hair is blown thin by winds of experience.
And there is so much knowledge and wisdom in

our heads, our heads can't hold it all.
It has to trickle down through
the rest of our bodies.
That's why we get thicker as we age.

Mary Rose had one other helpful thing to say to
older women, particularly her friends when they
began to walk like the old ladies they were. Mary
Rose would simply say, SHIT.

It was not the expletive; it was a posture-
improving directive. It stood for:
Shoulders back\
Head high
Eyes (**I**'s) straight ahead
Tummy tucked in.

When Mary Rose said it, for a short time all four
girls had excellent posture.

With all her loves, Mary Rose also loved the furry
body asleep in the back of the van parked in the
handicapped space back of Marks Bistro.

Geoffrey the Mastiff---
was sleeping so soundly he didn't realize his legs
were twitching. He was running really fast in
his dream and his long legs and big paws were
keeping up. He was chasing a squirrel.

Geoffrey the Mastiff hated squirrels.

A lot of times when they walked around the
grounds of their retirement community, Wiley
would take Geoffrey off his leash so he could go
after a squirrel. He could tree those little suckers
in no time, even though he was old now. In his
dream though, he was not old. He was a young,
superdog and it was as if he were wearing a black
cape and stick-up ears and playing Batdog.

Geoffrey was totally happy and content.

He knew his people were inside at Marks and he
would soon have some good people food to enjoy.
The servers at Marks knew Geoffrey because he
lay, perfectly behaved, at Mary Rose's feet on the
patio when it was patio weather. The servers,
year-round, put a little extra on Mary Rose's plate
for the loyal friend who was waiting for them, in
the van or on the patio.

It was not patio weather today.

The sky looked threatening, the leaves were blowing around the van, and there was just a little autumn nip in the air.

Geoffrey didn't care.

He was old now. He had been Mary Rose's dog – well, he belonged to all of them, but if he HAD to choose, he would lay by Mary Rose and cover her feet with his warm chest.

They met seven years ago when the wicked Busch family from Florida bought Meadow Lakes and the big mastiff had been the Busches' entire security system. He had been meaner then. Now, he only looked mean.

Back then he loved the smell of Mary Rose's Estee Lauder make-up, and knew she was scared to death of him.

He stalked her.

She hid from him.

He won.

He cornered her one day, forced her to step backward until she fell onto a couch, jumped on her, tipped over the couch, put his big paws on each side of Mary Rose and licked off all her make-up.

From that time on, Geoffrey the Mastiff had belonged to Mary Rose McGill.

Now he, like his people, was old. The vet guessed him to be eleven or twelve and each time he saw Geoffrey, reminded whoever brought him for his checkup that this was an unusually old age for a big dog.

Geoffrey realized things had changed.

He walked as slow as Wiley now.

The squirrels always had a head start.

And what seemed strange; when they got into the van or the Hummer, he needed a boost up to get in, even when the running board was down. And sometimes, when Raven was with them, the Indian just picked him up and lifted him out.

Funny.

He was still, like Alphonso and Raven, huge. He was still sharp, but he didn't hear well. It didn't matter. He didn't know that, just his people did.

He knew Mary Rose patted him sometimes and talked in her super soft voice and then she had water come out of her eyes. "Goodbye Soon," she would say. He didn't know who Goodbye Soon was, but he didn't like him. He made Mary Rose sad.

Geoffrey was happy, too, because he had a new adventure going. There was this very small human (he thought he was human) who wore dark boots with shiny buckles. He wore a funny hat and he was not much taller than Geoffrey. When he led Geoffrey by his collar, they were almost the same size.

This little person was helping Geoffrey slip out at night.

He would come to whichever apartment that happened to be Geoffrey's home for the night, open the door and just stand there until the big dog padded out.

Then they would take a walk to the most fascinating and horrible place Geoffrey had ever seen or smelled.

And now, when they went there, they were bringing something back with them that belonged to Geoffrey and the tiny person.

Geoffrey liked the little person's clothes.

What his doggie eyes couldn't see was that they were all green.

Oh, the Hatfields and McCoys They were Feudin' Mountain Boys

"He's gone!"

Mary Rose McGill hurried once again across the dining room to table 12 where her three friends were enjoying a morning coffee. Geoffrey was close behind her, tongue hanging out, looking tired.

Her eyes were wide and wet, and she had the most frightened look imaginable on her face.

"He's gone!" she repeated.

"This sounds like a re-run of a bad television sit com," Hadley said. "We just watched that one when you rushed in with Dr. Dennis Deadlee."

"This sounds worse than that," Robbie added with a smile.

"Sit down and talk," Marge, the forever detective said; then she added, "honey," to soften her strictness.

Mary Rose sat and looked at Marge to help her.

Geoffrey sat, too, and kept his big eyes on Mary Rose.

"First, WHO is gone?"

"Say it's not another television dream boy," Robbie said. Hadley nodded and did a little eye roll.

"Shhhh," Marge said, hushing everyone.

Mary Rose looked around.

"Wiley," she said, a nervous, whispering tremor in her voice.

They looked at her.

"And-" Marge urged her to continue.

"And I can't find him," Mary Rose said.

They were all quiet for a minute.

Even Marge's cane, hanging on its spot on the back of her chair seemed to be listening and looking a little bored.

Mary Rose took a deep breath.

"He was watching TV, his favorite morning show, and I was in the shower. I heard voices, but I thought he had turned up the TV."

She looked at the girls who were all staring at her. "He's getting a little hard of hearing, you know."

"Welcome to the club," Hadley smiled.

"What?" Robbie joked.

"Go on," Marge urged, ignoring them.

"So, when I went into the living room, he wasn't there. I got dressed and I sat in front of the television for a long time – like fifteen minutes – and then I wondered if he had gone downstairs and met someone and had coffee or something, so I waited another fifteen minutes. Nothing."

They were looking at her, encouraging her, but no one was worried. This was getting to be the typical Mary Rose.

Marge nodded at her to continue.

"So, I called him."

"That was logical, Mr. Spock," Robbie said.

"And his phone rang in the kitchen. He hadn't taken his phone and Wiley always takes his phone."

They knew this was true.

"I called Alphonso and he hadn't seen him or talked to him. I went to the exercise room. He wasn't there, but Zed was, and he hadn't seen him either."

She looked around as if to add something important. "Zed has a new workout suit. It's putrid green like cheap vomit."

For just a second Robbie wondered if expensive vomit contained lobster or steak and had a fancy color name.

"I also went by the game room where the coffee machine and the jigsaw puzzles are, and he wasn't there, and no one there had seen him. I asked Megan at the reception desk and I asked Sheryl in her office and no one has seen him, so I thought he had probably gone home by this time, so I went home, and he wasn't there."

They waited while she caught her breath.

"So, you came down here," Hadley said.

"No, first I retraced my steps all over the place and asked everyone again and I took Geoffrey with me and said, 'Find Wiley,' but that didn't work. Geoff just wanted to go out, so I went out for a minute." She looked around. "It's getting cooler out."

"Then I thought that if maybe you girls were here, Wiley and Alphonso and Raven would be, too, and you just hadn't texted me. But they aren't here, and neither is Wiley."

Both were true - her observation of the dining room and her weather report.

Mary Rose McGill was a keen observer of the obvious.

"We'll track that man down," Marge said, and she pulled out her smart phone.

"Call Wiley Vondra," she told her phone.

They listened to it ring.

When it stopped, Marge called again, giving Wiley more than enough time to reach his phone from wherever he was. Once again, she heard Wiley's voice on his voicemail.

"Howdy. This is Wiley. Do your thing at the beep." No answer.

"He's somewhere," Hadley said.

"That is so profound," Robbie said.

They waited.

No one said anything, but both Mary Rose and Robbie, who faced the dining room doors, kept looking and watching the entrance from the hallway.

Hadley and Marge kept eyeing the grounds beyond the windows.

Time passed.

"Okay," Marge said.

She called Wiley again.

No answer.

She called Alphonso. "Alphonso, can you come to the dining room?"

When the big man arrived, they moved closer together so his scooter could park beside table 12.

"We can't find Wiley," Marge said.

Alphonso shrugged. "Call him," he said.

"No answer after a couple of calls and Mary Rose says he forgot his phone. She's been all over the place twice."

"I know she hit all our offices," Alphonso said, looking at Mary Rose.

Mary Rose was looking even more frightened and holding onto the table with both hands.

Robbie picked up her phone. "Call Raven," she told it.

In just minutes all six of them were sitting close together at table 12.

There are different kinds of snakes.

They went over all the possibilities again for Alphonso and Raven.

Finally, Alphonso sighed and looked at Raven. "How good are you at tracking?"

"I'm an Apache."

"I know that. I asked you how good you are at tracking."

"I am so good," the big Indian said. "And it comes from generations of good trackers."

He took a breath.

"My great uncle, Leaping Lizard was lying, flat on his stomach, face down, ear to the ground, when two white men road up on horses. They got off and looked at Leaping. My great uncle said, 'Conestoga wagon. Two oxen. Man driving. Woman sitting beside him holding a baby. Little girl in the back. Big dog trotting alongside.'

'Wow!' one of the men said. 'You can tell all that just putting your ear to the ground?'

'No,' my ancestor said. 'They just ran over me.'"

"Leaping Lizard?" Alphonso asked, his eyebrows raised.

Hadley groaned. Robbie did an eye roll. Alphonso grinned. Marge shook her head, Mary Rose just looked at her hands still gripping the table.

Raven thought for a minute.

They were all quiet.

"If Geoffrey wanted to go outside, he may not just have wanted to find a tree," Raven said. "He may have been trying to tell you where Wiley was." Raven reached down and put his hand on the mastiff. "Geoff. Want to go out?"

Geoffrey got to his feet, slipping a little on the dining room floor.

"Grab a jacket," Mary Rose said.

"Let's all grab jackets and go with him," Hadley said.

They all nodded.

"I'll get my canes," Alphonso said.

Marge grabbed hers off the back of her chair.

The breeze was gentle, the sun was out, and it was a good, fresh, autumn day. They went out the front door and Raven and Geoffrey walked around the outdoor parking lot twice. Then Raven moved the old dog onto the grass, knelt beside him, put his head to Geoffrey's head and didn't say anything, just knelt there for several minutes.

"What's he doing?" Mary Rose asked.

Robbie shrugged. It looked to her like Spock's Vulcan Mind Meld on Star Trek, but she had a pretty good idea just what Raven and Geoffrey were doing.

Alphonso spoke up. "He's giving the dog a sense of what he wants, It's an OAT."

"OAT?" Hadley and Mary Rose said together.

"That's oat – like the grain," Hadley added.

"It stands for Old Apache Trick," Robbie put in. "I've seen it before."

She may have seen it before, but what was happening to Robbie right then was anything but pleasant. She had a Marie LaVeau feeling that something terrible had happened. Something **really** terrible, and she could feel her hands grow colder, and not from the autumn weather. She grasped them together and held them to her chest.

Raven stood up, and he and Geoffrey began to walk slowly over the grounds at the edge of Meadow Lakes. Geoffrey wasn't on his leash, but he was so close to Raven's leg he seemed to touch the Indian's black jeans.

They walked slowly, Raven not saying a word. The friends watched until Raven and Geoff turned a corner and started around the side of the building; then they slowly, and quietly, followed. Robbie's hands were still clasped to her chest, making her a little off balance as she walked. Their feet crunched in the leaves. More leaves drifted around them and they moved as if in slow motion toward Raven and his dog, for now Geoffrey was obviously one with the tall man next to him.

On the far side of the Meadow Lakes building, Raven and Geoffrey stopped. They were looking across a small field where an old, almost extinct road had once run along one side.

"What is over there?" Raven asked as Alphonso came up beside him.

Alphonso was balancing on his canes, breathing a little heavily.

"An old farmhouse," Alphonso said.

Part of the roof of the farmhouse could be seen from where they were standing.

Marge moved up next to them and stood on the other side of Geoffrey. "A ramshackle old house near the farmhouse used to be the headquarters and home of four witches. They were the ones who killed Percolator Rasmussen eight years ago, and that killing is what brought me to Meadow Lakes."

Raven looked around for Mary Rose.

"Mary Rose, has Wiley said anything about anyone who might want to do him harm?"

Robbie froze. Grandma LaVaeu was right inside of her.

She trembled a little.

Mary Rose thought. "No – everything was fine."

Robbie shook her head, so slightly no one except Raven noticed.

They stood looking out over the field at the roof of the farmhouse.

"Who has he talked about lately?" Marge asked, leaning on her cane.

Mary Rose thought some more.

"He was thinking about an old relative last week. He read a newspaper and he said, 'Oh, he's out of jail. I may see him or his mother.' Then he added, 'I think his mother's dead.'"

"Did he say who it was?" Raven asked.

They looked at Mary Rose.

When Mary Rose thought, she thought hard. "It was kind of a familiar name." She looked intense with all the hard thinking. "It was a relative he'd talked about who hated his side of the family and held a grudge, now that I remember it."

She looked around at them.

"It was a woman's name. Anna…. Anna." Then she brightened as she remembered.

"Anna Aconda!"

"Oh, Sweet Jesus," Robbie said. Her hands dropped to her sides. She did an eye roll and shook her head. She hadn't expected that.

"An Anaconda is a snake!" Robbie said.

"That's right!" Mary Rose said excitedly. "Wiley said they were all a family of snakes!"

The breeze picked up and stirred some dry leaves around their feet.

"I think we need to go to the farmhouse," Raven said.

Geoffrey, too, was looking off into the distance toward the farmhouse. If he had been a hound he would have been pointing.

Alphonso looked at the distance across the field. It had a slight slope that ended in front of the trees that surrounded the area. The old road was too deteriorated for any travel.

"That field's not big, but I think I'll go get the scooter."

Marge nodded agreement.

Alphonso was only gone a couple of minutes. He came out the side door, the green machine nearly smoking with speed. He stopped in front of Marge and she struggled onto the bitch seat. That exercise was not recommended for bad knees. She settled in, the tires complained, and the scooter sank into the ground an inch or two.

"Lucky the ground is hard," she said, putting her arms as far around Alphonso as she could reach.

He nodded and squinted toward the farmhouse.

They took off across the field, a rather pitiful and comical army of the elderly, intent on a rescue mission if it came to that.

They were all looking straight ahead, so no one saw the tiny man in green duck from where he was watching them from a third story window at the end of the hall at Meadow Lakes. He headed down the stairs and toward a side door.

Marge held on tightly to her cane, its tip firmly against her foot as they bounced along.

Alphonso's canes were strapped onto the side of the scooter in a custom-made container.

At least, Marge thought, I'm fully armed, and she knew how to use every jewel on that red cane. She held on tight to Alphonso as well.

Raven led the way, with Geoffrey just a couple of feet in front of him. The old dog seemed to know exactly where he was going.

He was going to find his Wiley.

This was HIS parade.

No grazing animal or person had served as steward of the field for years.

Raven and Geoff may have started out in the lead, but the green machine, groaning under the weight of Alphonso and Marge, soon bounced past them. It looked as if passing them in the scooter was not intentional. It looked as if Alphonso, who could handle anything, was having trouble handling the green machine on the rough field.

Robbie and Hadley were holding hands; partly to keep their balance and partly because Hadley had trouble seeing any holes or clods in the unmowed grass. Mary Rose, like the scared little rabbit she was, literally hopped along close to the leaders. It took longer than they thought it would, but finally hey made it across the field.

Marge realized she had been holding her breath. Alphonso realized he had been holding his breath, too, and his hands hurt from his tight grip on the steering bars of the scooter.

Robbie was out of breath. Her heart was beating faster than she liked to admit.

Hadley's eyes hurt from the sun and she had twisted an ankle when she stepped on a dirt clod that was so well-hidden Robbie didn't see it.

Mary Rose was praying she didn't have to pee, and Geoffrey, even though his legs hurt, was as attentive as the Apache beside him.

They stopped at the edge of the field.

A narrow, unkept dirt road separated the field from a weather-beaten, broken-down, battered little house that was falling apart. A chimney lay on the ground, broken to pieces. A part of the porch had fallen in, and one side wall was bowed out, ready to collapse. Every windowpane was shattered and broken.

"Who lived here?" Raven asked, looking at Marge.

"The four witches who did in poor old Percolator; Mabel, Myrtle, Mildred and Fred."

"Fred?" Raven asked, his eyebrows raised.

"It was officially Milifred, but she didn't like it."

Raven nodded.

"They were sisters," Marge added as a footnote.

The farmhouse could be seen through three rows of trees that grew between it and the little house. Since the leaves were gone from the trees, they could make out several doors and windows and a weather-battered shed. The shed was next to what appeared to be a more modern garage.

While the little house was falling apart, the farmhouse, though it had not been occupied for years, had remained in reasonably good condition. They stood and looked at it.

"I'm tired," Hadley said. "Old age is coming at a really bad time."

Robbie agreed. "And look at Raven. He looks so young and energetic when he's excited like this."

Hadley nodded. "He looks younger than we do and he's the same age we are." She thought for a minute. "Very few women admit their age. Very few men look it."

"Sucks," Robbie nodded.

From the top of the field, the little man in green climbed onto a tree stump and watched them talking together on the other side of the field.

Without saying a word, Raven and Geoffrey began to walk slowly toward the trees that bordered the farmhouse.

Getting across the old road was a challenge, and Hadley's ankle began to ache.

The scooter bounced so high Marge's butt flew two inches off the seat. When she landed back down, the tires sank another inch into the ground.

"Damn!" Alphonso said.

On the other side of the road was a ditch six or seven inches deep and about a foot wide.

"Oh, great," Alphonso said.

He climbed off the scooter and helped Marge dismount.

"Maybe all of you should stay here while Geoffrey and I go and check it out," Raven said.

"Not me!" Mary Rose said loudly, and she moved up next to Geoffrey, who leaned against her leg in sympathy.

"I don't see all that well," Hadley said. "With any luck I could bump into the villain we're looking for and solve the whole mystery."

Robbie, who was still feeling her grandmother Marie close to her simply said, "I have to go."

She gave Raven a sad, long look and he understood.

"Marge and Alphonso?" Raven asked, looking at them holding their canes.

"Get a life, Kemosabe!" Marge said.

"You want me to put you on the ground like I used to on the football field?" Alphonso added.

They started across the ditch, Alphonso leaning heavily on his canes, Marge close by him, still leaning on her red cane as well. She wanted to stay close to him in case he fell or needed help, then admitted that it would probably be she who would fall or need help. This growing old really does come at a bad time –sometimes more so than others. This was one of those times.

Hadley and Robbie made their way across the ditch together. Holding on to each other, Hadley being very careful with every step, Robbie wondering what Grandmother Marie could do to help and how to use the LaVaeu talent if she had it.

Mary Rose, suddenly more limber than they had seen her in years, hurried along beside Raven, who pulled her up the steep other side of the ditch.

She started off into the trees that lined the road and partially hid the farmhouse.

Geoffrey was panting and limping a little, but Mary Rose was by his side, so he felt good. It was mighty fine to be outside and free and he knew that somehow, they were on a mission and it involved finding his Wiley.

Only Raven didn't seem affected by what was going on. He looked around to check on the others and seeing them make good, or reasonably good, progress, he picked up his pace and was soon lost in the trees.

What no one saw, since they were so focused on the path ahead, was the small person in green with the shiny black boots hurrying not far behind them as they started down the hill. He hopped along, his top hat bouncing up a few inches off his head as he hopped, his gold chain flying up and down against his vest.

There was a happy, hopeful smile on his rugged little face.

Part way down the hill, just as the awkward little party ahead of him got across the ditch and headed into the line of trees, he tripped and fell flat. Instead of getting to his feet, he turned onto his side and rolled, holding onto his hat and bouncing over the clods, rolling over and over all the way to the bottom. A rabbit, who had found herself in his way, jumped into the air, turned a somersault and triple-hopped to safety.

He rolled directly into the bottom of the ditch, lay still for a few seconds, then rolled over, grabbed hold of a root sticking out of the ground and pulled himself up. Another root helped him get to the top of the ditch. He stood, hands on hips, and looked through the trees at the farmhouse.

He could see the backs of the other tall people standing together, looking up at the windows on the second floor.

When A Body Meets A Body

As they slipped through the trees, Raven held out his arms for them to stop. They stepped back into the line of trees and waited. The farmhouse was two-stories high, there were windows across the back on both floors, and they immediately noticed two other things: the curtains were drawn across all the windows and there was smoke curling skyward out of the chimney.

"If this place has been abandoned for years, why is smoke coming out of the chimney?" Marge asked.

She had moved up beside Raven and was looking at all the closed and curtained windows. Alphonso was beside her, leaning less heavily on his canes now that the ground was level.

Raven gave a small nod.

"Stay here out of sight," he said, turning toward them. "Geoff and I are going to do a little reconnoitering and if we all go, anyone in the house is likely to notice."

"Why you?" Mary Rose asked. "I notice stuff."

"Because I'm bigger than you, I'm stealthy and I'm an Indian."

Mary Rose shrugged. It was clear the Apache left no room for arguments.

Raven and Geoffrey took off, darting quickly to the side of the house, then around the corner, all the while hugging the wall.

From their hiding place among the trees, the friends could see a double garage on one side of the house and a large, well-worn tool shed near it, not far from the house. Car tracks led in and out of the garage.

"It's been used recently," Robbie observed, nodding toward the car tracks.

Robinson Leary, ace detective.

There was no wind. The day was as quiet as death.

"You know what?" Hadley whispered. "We are at an age when work is less fun, and fun is more work."

"You think this is fun?" Mary Rose squeaked. They all looked at her and said, "Shhhh."

Hadley decided not to try to explain, but she could remember when crossing a little field, climbing a ditch and having an adventure had, indeed, been fun.

And, she also supposed if Wiley turned out to be inside, sharing an early morning shot of bourbon with a long-lost relative, Mary Rose would have a full-blown tizzy fit.

That was a better scenario than Hadley's other thought: that the Aconda family Wiley had mentioned had shown up, kidnapped him and were holding him in the farmhouse.

Explained the smoke coming from the chimney.

Her other thought was one she wouldn't let herself entertain: that the Acondas had shown up, all right, and that Wiley was dead.

She shook her head and refused to think that. She turned toward Robbie and knew she was thinking the same thing.

Raven and Geoff circled the farmhouse, still hugging the walls, Raven making a good try at peeking in the curtained windows, and Geoffrey sniffing along the foundation. Even with the leaves covering the ground, the friends could hear no footsteps as Raven moved stealthily and surely. He was moving quickly, but time seemed to have slowed to a frightening crawl. Mary Rose was rubbing her hands together and moving from one foot to the other. Hadley wondered if she had to pee.

Geoffrey got back to them before Raven. He went to Mary Rose, sat beside her and leaned his big, awkward frame against her leg. She took a short step to stay on balance.

"There is someone inside," Raven said as he slipped up beside them. "I could hear a television when I was outside what must be the living room.

I was able to get onto the porch without being heard. I could hear it through the front window but couldn't see anything."

A large porch ran along the entire wall on the front of the house. They were standing at the rear of the house but could see one of the pillars from where they stood.

"There is a small, and I do mean small, window broken out in the basement on the other side, but it's way too small for any of us to crawl through." He looked back at the house. "One more thing. When we were on the other side, Geoffrey stopped cold, sat his Olympic sit and stared at a second-floor window. I stood with him for a minute. No curtain on that window, and a huge oak tree with a big branch that brushes up against the glass. I don't think there was a squirrel up there to attract a dog's attention. When I said, 'Wiley?' Geoff's tail started to wag, and he kept staring at that window. I think Wiley is in that room, which is no doubt an upstairs bedroom."

Hadley looked at Robbie. "That's the most I've ever heard him say at one time," she whispered.

Raven gathered them in close. "Let's go over to that window and see what Geoffrey tells us. Stay quiet."

They began to move, silently, stealthily, almost tree to tree, until they reached the other side of the house. For several yards they would be exposed, but the oak tree Raven had mentioned was huge, one branch tight against a second-floor window. All six of them and Geoffrey could hide behind its massive trunk. Not far from the tree was the tool shed. The shed leaned a little to one side, as if the winter winds had not been kind to it.

Crunch. Crackle. Crunch.

The leaves seemed loud under their feet. Hadley found herself moving on her tiptoes and Robbie found herself drawn strongly toward the window that was reflecting sunlight like an eye above them.

They stood shoulder-to-shoulder, almost pressed against the big tree. Beautiful red oak leaves fell gently around them, and Hadley thought how lovely it would be under different circumstances. She could see how good a picnic table would look in the shade of this giant, and how at one time there might have been a tire swing hanging from that huge branch that reached out above them and crunched against the window.

Robbie moved over next to Raven and slipped her arm through his. "This is the place," she whispered. He nodded.

As they stood looking at the window, it slowly and with a soft scraping noise, opened.

There was no one there.

They stared up at the now open window.

They waited.
Nothing.

"Holy crap," Marge said.

"Sweet Jesus," Robbie said.

"Did I just hear the window open?" Hadley said.

"Wiley!" Mary Rose yelled.

Raven clapped his hand over her mouth. "Sorry."

Alphonso just stood and stared at the window, shaking his head.

Nothing happened.

There was no movement or sound around that second-story window. Even the breeze had quieted.

Geoffrey was staring at the window with them. Suddenly, the silence was broken by a loud bark. "Geoffrey! Shhhh!" Mary Rose said.

They stood stock still, waiting to hear a door bang open or for someone to appear around the corner carrying a shotgun.

Hadley realized she was holding her breath. Marge realized she was holding her cane in rifle position.

Three or four minutes dragged by.

The breeze stirred their hair.

Leaves fell around them.

Still nothing.

"We need to get to that window," Alphonso said. Raven nodded.

Mary Rose nodded more vigorously.

"You can climb up this tree, go out on that limb and look inside," Mary Rose said, taking hold of Raven's arm.

Raven looked surprised.

"You're an Indian," Mary Rose explained, giving him the, "You're a total idiot," look.

"I'm an Indian," Raven said, a slight smile settling across his lips. "I'm not a dumb Indian."

Mary Rose gave him an angry look, hesitated for just a minute, then turned and hurried toward the tool shed.

They watched her.

She disappeared inside, took only a minute, and reappeared lugging a huge ladder behind her.

The end of the ladder burrowed into the leaves covering the ground as she drug it behind her.

Mary Rose was struggling and wrestling with the long, rung-filled monster.

Robbie turned, hurried toward her and grabbed the side of the ladder several ladder rungs behind Mary Rose. They staggered just a bit as they maneuvered the long, heavy thing toward the tree. Hadley, Marge, Raven and Alphonso stared, as if they were frozen to the ground where they stood.

Mary Rose and Robbie didn't ask for any help. Together they stood the ladder up against the tree and balanced it. The top of the ladder reached to three feet below the massive branch.

Marge looked at Alphonso. "They just strong-armed a twelve-foot ladder."

He nodded. "Impressive."

The ladder leaned against the tree, bowing a little in the middle. Half-way up a rung was missing. It looked like a refugee from a 1950's elopement gone wrong.

They watched as Mary Rose did her best to get the ladder into the most stable position. It didn't move. After two gallant attempts, she took two steps backward, grabbed a deep breath and walked bravely to the ladder, put one foot on the bottom rung and began to climb.

"Mary Rose, wait!" Robbie said as loudly as she dared.

"No!" Hadley croaked, even louder.

"Oops," Marge said as Mary Rose slipped a little on the third rung.

"Don't do that!" Alphonso rasped at a determined Mary Rose McGill.

Raven put his hands on his hips and shook his head.

"Shit!" he said, and he reached around Mary Rose's waist and lifted her, kicking and squirming, off the ladder and planted her firmly on the ground.

"Shit again!" he said, and he started up the ladder. He turned his head when he reached the fourth rung. "Stay!" he said to Mary Rose.

She stayed and Geoffrey, standing right beside her, sat at the command.

The old piece of wood bowed further inward and the top banged against the tree every time Raven reached a new rung.

Raven was halfway up the ladder when Hadley realized she was holding her breath again. She looked around. Robbie was turned away, her eyes closed as if in prayer. Marge and Alphonso were under the ladder holding it firmly against the tree.

Mary Rose was flat on her butt on the ground. Geoffrey was in the same position beside her.

Hadley didn't remember Raven pushing her down, but she had landed with her legs spread out, her arms behind her, head raised to the large figure making his way up the tree. Geoffrey was in full sit beside her, looking up just like Mary Rose. Both of them were doing a good 'stay'.

Hadley moved over in front of Mary Rose and offered her a hand up. Mary Rose took it and struggled up. With her other hand, she brushed off her jeans.

No one said a word.

Marge kept an eye on the house, listening for a front door to slam and someone unpleasant to come around the corner fully armed and not happy. Her hand gripped her cane in a position making it ready for use.

When Raven got to the space between the ladder and the branch, he stopped. He looked down at them.

They silently looked up at him.

Robbie opened her eyes, her mouth grim and firmly set.

The Indian shrugged.

"I track. I climb," he said, and he grabbed the branch with both hands.

There was a communal intake of breath as Raven pushed back, lifted himself and swung one leg over the branch.

The ladder swung away from the tree and began to fall backward, directly onto Mary Rose and Geoffrey. The big dog made large and fast paw prints sideways. Mary Rose stepped to one side as fast as she could. Hadley was glad she had helped her to her feet. There was a loud crash as the ladder landed flat on the ground.

It missed Mary Rose by inches.

They stood as if paralyzed.

Not a sound from them and not a sound from the farmhouse.

"Whew," Robbie said, and they all let out their breath.

Marge, Hadley and Alphonso all got to the ladder at the same time, grabbed ahold of the sides and lifted it up and against the tree once more, moving it to the exact spot where it had been. It leaned heavily against the trunk.

As they looked up into the tree, they saw Raven, safe and secure on the gigantic branch, except for one thing.

He was facing the wrong direction.

He was looking into the trunk of the tree and not the window.

He had thrown his right leg, which was his strongest, over the branch, pulled himself up, and ended up face-to-face with an angry squirrel that clung to the trunk.

The squirrel scolded.

Raven lunged toward it and the squirrel darted up to a higher branch.

Robbie looked at Hadley and they both smiled. Marge shook her head.

Mary Rose sat back down, and Geoffrey sat beside her.

Alphonso smiled and looked up at his friend. "The goal post is in the opposite direction," he said as loud as he dared.

Raven shrugged, pulled his left leg around, moved his whole body and rotated to face the window, which was still wide open.

He slowly began to inch along the branch, still sitting down and straddling it.

"Didn't look very dignified," Marge said to Hadley.

"And I've never seen Raven be awkward before."

"He's been having trouble with a hip," Robbie chimed in, keeping her voice low. "He blames it on a football hit from Alphonso."

Hadley nodded. She was beginning to feel as if they had been here for a long time, way too long. Geoffrey presented his opinion by pulling himself up from his sitting position, walking slowly over to the tree, lifting a leg and peeing a long stream onto the roots.

Alphonso was still looking up at Raven, who was slowly going butt-lift by butt-lift toward the window. The branch, while big, swayed a little. "The odds of his making it to the window are about the same as my winning the lottery," the old football buddy said.

Mary Rose got up, went to the tree and looked up. "Be careful of Wiley, Raven. If he is in there be sure you help him out. Be sure he doesn't fall. Be sure he's okay." She looked pitiful.

Raven didn't buy it. "Mary Rose," he whispered loud enough so she could hear, "I'm up here to save his ass, not kiss it."

Mary Rose gasped.

Alphonso smiled.

Hadley, Marge and Robbie smiled.

Hadley added an eye roll.

Geoffrey sat.

Raven worked his way slowly over a smaller branch sticking out of the main branch on which he was sliding. He was still sitting down, inching his way forward. "Some days I don't have a sufficient supply of Apache cuss words to meet my needs," he mumbled to himself. He thought about what he said as he made his next slide.

"Now I'm starting to sound like some damn white man."

The main branch had grown up against the house and had been sawed off years ago. Now, once again, it was pushing against the wall just beneath the window.

Raven worked his way, butt-slide by butt-slide to the open window. "This is not fitting an Apache warrior," he said to himself as he put one hand against the windowsill. He lifted himself up as high as he could with his legs still tight on each side of the branch and peered into the window. He shook his head at what he saw.

Lying on his back, spread-eagled, his hands and feet tied to the head and foot of the bed, another rope around his waist that traveled totally around the mattress, was Wiley Vondra. He was wearing jeans, a flannel shirt, his brown vest, he still had his brown cowboy boots securely on his feet and his mouth was taped shut with duct tape. Wiley's hat was perched on his face, hiding his eyes.

Raven couldn't tell if he was alive, dead, or unconscious.

"Wiley!" Raven whispered as loudly as he could.

Then out loud he said, "Wiley Vondra!"
No answer, no movement.

Raven looked at the group standing, or in Mary Rose and Geoffrey's case, sitting, below him.

"He's in here!" he said, a rasp to his whisper.

Then, without another word, the big Indian grabbed ahold of either side of the window, pulled himself up and put his right leg over the windowsill and into the room. His other leg followed, and in just minutes he was inside, looking down at his friend.

Wiley was breathing, that much Raven could tell. He lifted the hat. Wiley's eyes were closed.

Raven gave him a gentle shake.

"Wiley!" he whispered, again as loudly as he could.

No response.

"Wiley!" Raven said out loud, and he shook Wiley even harder.

Wiley's eyes popped open.

"Mhmmmhm!!" he said, and pointed to the tape covering his mouth.

Raven pulled it off in one fast yank.

"Ow!" Wiley said.

He struggled with his ropes, and Raven pulled a mean-looking knife out of his pocket and flipped it open.

In less than a minute, Wiley Vondra was free.

"Unconscious?" Raven asked as Wiley ran his hand through his hair, looked dazed and settled his Stetson firmly on his head.

"Asleep," Wiley responded. "It gets boring laying here."

Raven pointed to the window. "Let them know you're okay."

Wiley went to the window and looked out, surprised to see the crowd gathered under the tree.

Everyone below waved a little wave, nodded and smiled.

Mary Rose began to cry, turned onto her hands and knees and struggled to her feet.

Geoffrey barked and Alphonso slammed the dog's mouth shut with one hand.

"Shhhhh!" the four women said together.

Geoffrey's eyes got big and he Shhhhhhed.

In the upstairs bedroom, Raven sat on the bed and motioned for Wiley to sit beside him.

"Talk," Raven said.

"I was watching *Adam 12* on TV and Mary Rose was in the shower. Next thing I know, there's a gun poking me in the ribs from behind and a bag over my head. Nobody said anything. Somebody pulled me up and started leading me out the door. Some other bastard started pushing me from behind. I tried to yell, but they pushed the gun farther into my ribs and anyway, the shower was running and what could Mary Rose do? They had a car parked right outside the side door. On the lawn. Motor running. They pushed me into the back seat and brought me here."

"Who?" Raven asked.

"Oh, the Acondas. My family's arch enemies. We have a long-time, standing feud going on that's right up there with the Hatfields and McCoys."

"How many?"

"Four. Ron, Don, Con and George."

"Ron Aconda, Don Aconda, Con Aconda and George?"

"Different fathers."

Wiley rubbed his wrists where the ropes had been. "Trouble with the Acondas is they are so ugly. When you fight with somebody who's ugly and you beat 'em to a pulp, it don't make any difference. They look just like they looked to begin with."

Wiley was sitting on the bed beside Raven.

There was nowhere else in the room to rest your derrière. The room was way past stark. The walls were grey. The wood in the floor was grey. The bedspread was grey, and the dirt on the windows made the glass grey. Sun could penetrate, but it was not worth the effort.

Raven and Wiley sat side-by-side talking while everyone outside looked at their watches, checked their phones and waited.

"Who is here now?" Raven asked.

"Damned if I know. I've been asleep and last I heard was a door slam and the television come on."

They could hear the television faintly from downstairs.

Raven stood, moved silently to the door and opened it. The television sound increased.

He moved slowly to the top of the stairs, and without making a sound, slipped stair by stair downward until he could see through the banisters to the room below.

He was looking at a large living room which was, surprise, surprise, grey. Walls and floor were grey and along one wall, exactly underneath where Raven was standing on the stairs. was a large sectional. The upholstery was grey, worn and dirty. Pizza boxes and empty beer bottles were strewn over the floor. The dirt on the windows matched the dirt upstairs.

Raven was absolutely quiet.

A bird lifted its voice outside, calling for food.

Red leaves blew against the window.

Across from the sectional was a 55-inch television with a cable hookup. Seated on the sectional was a man who went far beyond the ugly Wiley had mentioned. The television was blaring out an old replay of a *Gunsmoke* episode.

Raven remained quiet. There would be no trouble.

Raven could easily troubleshoot the situation. The problem with trouble is it usually shoots back.

What needed to be done would be done quietly.

What Raven could see of the man below him, made him smile. If this came to a battle of wits, the man on the sectional was definitely not armed. He looked like a refugee from *Duck Dynasty.* He was thin, wore old denim coveralls, a long-sleeve white flannel shirt and was in his stocking feet. No shoes in sight. One shoulder strap of the coveralls had slipped down over his elbow.

Raven looked for a long time at his long, straggly beard, which of course was grey. His denim coveralls were so old they were grey. Only his white shirt stood out from the bland upholstery. He seemed to be sound asleep.

So much for the on-going excitement of Matt, Doc and Miss Kitty.

Raven moved quietly back up the stairs.

Other than one small, wimpy creak, the stairs cooperated. He slid into Wiley's temporary bedroom and sat down beside him on the bed.

"Just one downstairs. Asleep. Have a plan."

"Now you're talking Indian again," Wiley complained.

Raven smiled.

He picked up a limp pillow off the head of the bed; the only pillow, and fluffed it up as best he could. He guessed it had been stuffed with feathers from chickens raised here, on this farm. Stuffed at a time nearly one hundred years ago when all parts of the chicken were used and feathers made a full, wonderful pillow or feather tick that kept you warm and comfortable all night, even on the coldest winter ones.

"We're going to slip downstairs. Keep quiet. Sneak up on the man. You smash the pillow up against his face and hold it while I do an Apache choke hold or smash his head in so we can escape."

Raven gave Wiley a questioning look.

"Sounds like a plan," he said. "Do whichever is easiest. Just remember, these guys are tough and stupid." Then he got philosophical. "I thought I might die here. When you're dead, you don't know you're dead, it just causes pain to the ones around you. Same when you're stupid."

Raven looked at him.

"Let's go," Wiley said, and he led the way quietly out the door into the grey and dusty hall. There was so much dust on the floor, he could make out the prints from Raven's boots when he had made the trip minutes before.

They slipped down the steps, hugging the wall to avoid squeaks, pausing on each step, then crossed over to the banister where they could stand in front of the sleeping man on the sectional. Wiley had a death grip on his pillow.

"He's not asleep," Wiley said out loud. "That's Con Aconda, and he's not asleep. He's passed out." He motioned to the beer-can covered floor. "His work."

Raven nodded.

Wiley thought for a minute.

"I don't want to tell everybody outside that we just walked out," Wiley smiled. He took four steps forward and smashed the pillow into Con Aconda's face. He held it there, still smiling.

Raven smiled back, then reached out with both hands, put one on Con's back, slid the other under the pillow, found the man's neck and did a slight twist. Con lifted one foot into the air, sighed, fell back and was quiet.

"Is he dead?" Wiley said, a hopeful note creeping into his question.

Raven shook his head.

"Makes a hell of a better story," Wiley said, still holding onto the pillow. "I say, never let the truth get in the way of a good story."

They turned and walked out the front door, just as any polite guests would do.

The porch gave a little under their feet as they hurried along it, hopped off the end and hurried to the group still patiently gathered around the tree.

Mary Rose saw Wiley first, gave a little yip. Geoffrey gave a little yip, and they both ran toward the man in the brown leather vest.

Raven was afraid Mary Rose was going to jump onto Wiley, wrap her legs around him and take him to the ground, so he moved quickly behind him to push him back upright if that happened. It didn't.

Mary Rose came to, if the ground had been wet, would have been a skidding stop, just in front of Wiley. She looked at him, tears streaming down her cheeks, grabbed him and instead of his falling backward, Raven became afraid he would be suffocated.

Wiley grabbed back.

"I know that at our age we're facing death every day," Mary Rose blurted out. "I just didn't want it to be now or be this way."

Wiley looked at Raven. "She wants me to die from marital over-exertion," he said.

Raven smiled.

As the group gathered around Wiley, a familiar sound reached them from the road they had all judged as impassable. Wiley gripped his pillow tighter.

"Car!" Raven said. "Head for the shed!"

Mary Rose had dashed into the shed to drag out the old wooden ladder. Now they had to leave the ladder leaning against the tree.

The shed was a great hiding place, even when Mary Rose said, as she began to hop alongside Wiley and Geoffrey--

"Oh. I forgot to mention. There's a dead body in the shed."

A Dead Body in the Shed

The old shed made the old house look like it was inhabited by Mr. Clean. Cobwebs hung from every window and covered the stacked and piled junk that was everywhere. There was so much dust and so many leaves on the floor that they could see Mary Rose's footprints and the drag marks from the ladder. In addition, he floor was covered with the tiny tracks of rodents who had been intent on building rodent condo and giving the little building a rich rodent smell.

Hadley took a deep breath that was really a gasp.

Geoffrey took a sniffing tour and loved the place.

They hurried inside, shut the door and crowded around the one window that faced the driveway. The dust was so thick on the window, they were pretty sure they wouldn't be seen.

An old monster truck with oversized tires rolled into the driveway just as they heard the click on the shed door lock. The door didn't lock, it just announced it was closed and did so with a tinny click.

"No road is impassable for that dude," Alphonso said, a touch of envy in his attitude.

"Those tires are so big you could set a VW bug inside the hubcap," Wiley said.

"Admirable," Raven added.

The girls could see the truck, too.

"Ridiculous," Hadley said.

"Tasteless," Robbie added, and did her own eye roll.

"Car cancer," Mary Rose said, speaking of the rust that had eaten holes on the old GMC mounted on the oversized tires.

The truck sat there for a few minutes.

"What's he doing?" Mary Rose whispered.

"If he were a woman, some smart-ass would say, 'Putting on makeup,'" Hadley said.

"I can see him." Marge added. "The driver is finishing a beer and there is another man beside him on the front seat.

They all took a step back when the truck doors opened. The men would have a high jump to the ground.

"Can they see the ladder?" Robbie asked.

Raven shook his head.

"I can't see really well, but I can see ugly and I bet they have ugly sleeves of tattoos, too," Hadley said. Squinting out the window.

She would have been right. Part of the tail of a snake tattoo showed on one man's neck, looking as if it were slithering down his arm.

The two men were both tall and thin, and like their brother inside, had long, straggly grey beards that covered the fronts of their shirts. The beards were thin, separated in places and looked as if they had never quite been worth the effort to grow them.

They both wore cheap brown work boots.

"Those boots are straight off the rack at Walmart," Wiley observed.

Their flannel shirts looked as if they hadn't seen a laundry room in months, and Robbie could make out long, red underwear at the necks of both shirts along with the parts of more tattoos.

They had long, greasy hair and wore feed store caps that sat too high on their heads.

The friends were quiet as death.

"Who?" Raven whispered to Wiley.

"Don and Ron," Wiley answered. "George doesn't seem to be anywhere around."

"I think George is around over here," Mary Rose said quietly.

She was standing by what appeared to be a pile of blankets and towels thrown up against the opposite wall. Several old pictures in oval frames were nailed on the wall, giving the shed a bizarre look of an antique showroom gone rouge.

Geoffrey was already pawing at the stack and whining a soft whine.

Robbie took a quick look around. The ancient family portraits were charming, cobwebs and all. What attracted her attention was a huge stack of books resting against one wall. They had obviously been used in a mouse-led housing project and water had damaged some.

She hurried over, ignoring everyone who was gathering around the pile of blankets and towels and George.

"Oh, my!" she said a little too loudly, "here's an old pulpit Bible in a wooden case and it's in excellent condition. This is a museum piece."

Hadley heard her and looked her way. On the wall above where Robbie was kneeling was a once-white board with decorative hooks holding what at one time had been a glorious collection of cast iron skillets. They were brown with rust now, but Hadley could tell that at one time they had been a country wife's prize cookware.

"Look above you," Hadley whispered to Robbie. She looked and smiled. Grandma Marie LaVeau was nowhere near Robinson Leary now. Robbie was lost in the adventure of books and cast-iron skillets.

Wiley was making his own discoveries. He pulled a blue tarp off a stack of wooden chairs that were stacked almost to the ceiling.

He pulled one out just as the door to the house closed behind the two newcomers.

The whole stack tumbled down.

The crash was like a direct hit from a tornado or of a time in the old radio show when a comedian named Fibber McGee opened his closet and everything fell out.

They froze.

Raven slipped quietly to the window and watched, his back pressed against the wall.

Nothing from the house.

He nodded.

The group moved slowly over the narrow floor toward the unpleasant pile of blankets where Mary Rose was standing.

"The ladder was right here," she said, pointing to a spot along the wall where the ladder had lain.

The marks of the sides could be seen in the dust. "So, when I grabbed it, one of these blankets caught on the top of the ladder and I saw this." She pointed down toward the remaining blankets and towels that made up the stack of discarded items.

Geoffrey's nose was burrowing into the pile.

Sticking out from beneath it all was an arm with a hand attached. The arm was wearing the exact clothes worn by the two men who just arrived, and as Raven noted, the same as Con, the one who was unconscious inside.

Wiley moved closer to Mary Rose, bent over and lifted two towels from the face attached to the body.

"George," he said.

"How did he die?" Hadley asked.

"How long has he been here?" Robbie asked. She looked at Hadley and with an impish grin, put one hand over her mouth. "Dead in the shed," she said.

Hadley grinned back and did an eye roll.

Mary Rose had the most intelligent question. "What the heck do we do now?"

Marge moved around to the side of the body. George's backside was tight up against the wall beneath a small window.

She bent over, her large rear demanding generous space from her friends surrounding her.

They stepped back and gave her generous space.

She felt for a pulse she knew she wouldn't find. She lifted the arm and let it drop. It landed with a soft, 'thud'. She looked at Raven and Wiley who were standing as close as possible to George's head.

"Take all this junk off him, will you?"

She looked around.

"And see if you can find me a friggin' chair."

She put her hand on her back and slowly and painfully straightened up.

Wiley hurried over to the downed stack of chairs and found Marge her friggin' chair, a sturdy one.

Raven removed the blankets and towels, threw them in a new heap behind him, and pulled George flat and close to Marge. She leaned forward in the chair and examined the corpse.

Geoffrey's nose examined it with her.

"Yuk," Mary Rose said.

"Ick," Hadley added.

Robbie did the eye roll this time and moved closer. She was glad Grandma Marie wasn't this interested in modern-day bodies. In fact, Grandma had never been god at resurrections.

"I'm thinking two things," Marge said, leaning back and looking up at them. "One, he died a natural death. There are no wounds or bruises I can see and it's not likely he was poisoned. Two, it's time to call the police."

She pulled out her cell phone and pressed the emergency button that went directly to 911.

Nothing.

She tried again.

Still nothing.

Hadley took out her phone, the newest and most expensive one and did the same thing.

Same nothing.

"Damned dead spot!" Alphonso said angrily.

Everyone but George had their cell phones out and were hitting 911. They looked like a bunch of teenagers in the food court at the mall.

"Remember when we used to wait until 7pm to call long distance because it was cheaper?" Wiley asked.

They all nodded.

"Whoa," Raven said. "We're going to have company."

The door to the house was opening and one of the Acondas was hurrying out, carrying something large and black that draped over his shoulder. It looked like a heavy plastic bag.

"Oh, geeze," Robbie said. "It looks like he's carrying a body bag."

"For George, no doubt," Wiley added, holding his pillow tighter.

"That's where they've been," Hadley guessed. "Out getting a body bag for George."

"We sure don't want it to be for one of us," Marge said. She got up off her chair. took a firm grip on her red cane and motioned Wiley, Raven and Alphonso to come stand beside her several feet back ad facing the door. She motioned for the other three girls to guard the entrance.

They knew what to do.

Robbie grabbed the big Bible in its wooden case.

Hadley took two of the biggest cast iron skillets off the wall.

Mary Rose stood ready, as if she was preparing to run a 5K race.

Geoffrey was beside her as much on point as he could be.

Before Wiley, Alphonso or Raven could protest, the shed door opened.

"Ron!" Wiley said loudly as the skinny man stepped through the door.

"Vondra!" the skinny man yelled back, looking as surprised as anyone could look.

He would have looked more surprised to see the girls, but before he could notice them, Hadley beaned him with all her might on the side of his head. Tiny flakes of rust bounced off the skillet and flew into the air.

"Ow!"

She hit him on the other side of the head with the other skillet, then again with the first one as if his head were a ball between two ping-pong paddles. Rust flakes were showing up in his grey hair.

"Ow! Ow! Ow!"

Robbie bonked him on top of the head with the heavy Bible box, then lifted it above her head and with all her might and slammed it down again.

Ron Aconda made no sound this time.

His eyes rolled back.

Mary Rose stepped forward as the man began to slump and gave him her Olympic groin kick. His slumping made the kick go a little to the right and her momentum dislocated his knee.

"Drat!" she said.

"Woof, snarl," Geoffrey said, grabbing hold of one of Ron's arms with a lock-jaw grip that made pit bulls look like wimps.

Ron still didn't say anything.

His eyes were rolled back, then they began to close.

He took a couple of staggering steps in the direction of the door.

Raven looked at Alphonso. "Should we help them?"

Alphonso looked at his friend and smiled. "I think they have it under control."

Before Alphonso finished speaking, Ron was on his knees, losing consciousness, and Marge was aiming her red cane at an area between his legs.

The taser zipped.

Ron was zapped.

He fell over onto his back from the force of the taser.

Another bad man bites the dust.

Wiley rushed forward, fell to his knees and smashed the pillow into Ron's face.

"I got him!" he yelled.

Raven and Alphonso looked at each other.

They didn't do eye rolls. If they did they would have to give up their "man cards."

Marge, holding her cane, Robbie, holding the Bible, Hadley with a skillet in each hand and Mary Rose re-tying her shoe, all looked at Wiley and did eye rolls together.

Raven was the first to move.

He stepped over to one corner of the shed and took a long, strong rope from a hanger pounded crookedly into the wall.

"Very convenient," he said. "Let's tie him to George, then we know he's not going to run off."

Never underestimate a burned out old broad or an aging football hero. Alphonso, using just one cane, took a few steps and stood over George's body.

He looked at a corner that contained only a large bucket and what was once a wash tub.

"Move that crap," he said, motioning with his head.

Wiley scurried to the corner, grabbed the bucket with one hand and the tub with the other and got them out of the way.

Alphonso took hold of George's arm, and with no effort at all, lifted him partway up and pulled him over to exactly where he wanted him, sat him upright ad kept him that way with one hand on his head.

"There," he said to Raven.

Raven nodded and with a similar movement, grabbed Ron's arm and lifted him close to his brother. The Indian knelt, put the two men back-to-back and tied the rope in a complicated design around their ankles, waists, wrists and necks.

"Wait," Hadley said. She picked up a ragged blanket from George's stack and ripped two long strips off it. "Gags," she said.

Raven tied one strip around and into Ron's mouth, He handed the other one back to Hadley. "I don't think George needs one," he smiled.

"Oh, right," Hadley said with a slight, almost embarrassed grin.

Wiley grabbed the blue tarp and spread it over the two men, who were more than securely tied.

"Decorative," Hadley said, looking at what appeared to be a statue beneath a tarp.

"Tasteful," Robbie added.

"Brilliant idea," Mary Rose said, looking lovingly at Wiley.

"Sweet Jesus," Marge said, stealing Robbie's favorite phrase.

"Now what?" Wiley asked, looking in Raven's direction.

"We wait," Raven said.

"Indians wait better than the rest of us," Robbie said, looking at Marge.

"Stakeouts are a bitch," Marge nodded.

They waited.

They drug old wooden kitchen chairs out of the chair corner and sat. Following Raven's instructions, they put the backs of the chairs against the wall next to the window facing the house. That way, anyone looking in the window would not be quite so likely to spot any of them tight against the wall.

Mary Rose stood up.

"I have to pee," she said. "I'll be right back."

Before anyone could stop her, she and Geoffrey were out the door and around the shed to the other side.

The group inside looked at each other.

"A girl's gotta do what a girl's gotta do," Robbie said.

Raven, Alphonso and Wiley grinned at each other. The three women held their breath. It had definitely been a breath-holding day.

In just minutes Mary Rose was back, slipping in the door just behind the big mastiff, who had found a big tree to his liking and peed along with Mary Rose.

"Now I've got to go," Wiley said. "I was in that bedroom a long time," and he hurried to the door.

"Old men with prostates," Robbie said.

"Bummer there's not an outhouse," Hadley said, deciding that she could hold it.

They were quiet.

Time passed.

Wiley slipped back inside.

Hadley wished there was a clock that ticked and struck the hour.

Two squirrels scolded.

A bird sang a song to the heavens.

Leaves blew against the window across from them.

"Wind's from the west," Wiley observed, then added. "Don or Con have got to come check on Ron pretty soon."

"It will be Don," Raven said. "Con is still out cold." He reached over and took Robbie's hand. She was sitting as close to him as possible.

"What is this feud about, Wiley?" Mary Rose asked.

"Property," Wiley said. "It's always about property or women and this is both."

He looked at all of them looking back at him.

"My grandpappy, Vorhese Vondra," he looked at Robbie.

"Vorhese is a good name," she smiled back.

"Ahhhchooo!!" Hadley sneezed so loud they jumped.

"Dust," Mary Rose observed.

Hadley nodded.

"My grandpappy, Vorhese," Wiley continued, "lived next door to the Acondas in this little piss-ant town in the sand hills. One street. Didn't even have stop signs back then. No cars, just horses and buggies. The first Anna Aconda – these boys' mother is Anna Junior – and grandpappy had an affair while Anna was married to Cornelius Aconda."

"Skip the names, buddy," Alphonso said.

"Well, the affair was part of the feud. It really came to a head when Cornelius built a fence between his property and grandpappy's. He built the fence six inches on his own property but then he fought with grandpappy, saying it was on grandpappy's land."

"Did they have it surveyed?" Marge asked.

"Sure," Wiley said. "The survey said it was six inches on Aconda's land, but he didn't believe it. So, they stood on each side of the fence, cussed each other out and argued."

He smiled.

"Then the action began. They were in the local tavern on Saturday night. See, in this little town the thing to do was go into town on Saturday night, go to the grocery store, then stop at the tavern. Well, the tavern was full this Saturday, like always. Anna and Cornelius were there and so was Grandpappy. Anna was a big woman, and I mean big. She was telling this bunch gathered around the bar about having phlebitis and edema in her legs." He looked at them again and nodded at Robbie.

"Phlebitis is inflammation of the deep veins in the legs and edema is one heck of a lot of water in the tissue," Robbie said, getting into her professor mode.

Wiley nodded. "So, one of the ladies, in all innocence, asks Anna if she's ever been bed-ridden. And Anna looks at Grandpappy and says, 'Several times in bed and twice in the buggy.' That's when the fight started."

"Even when we were kids, we'd fight, and we'd fight mean, and the Acondas were so stupid. One time when Con was in Lincoln, Nebraska, a cop pulled him over. The cop said, 'Step out.' Con said, 'I can't, I'm too drunk. You get in.'"

Marge smiled. "Sometimes someone comes into your life unexpectedly and makes your heart race and changes everything. We call those people cops."

"Now when I drink responsibly, it means I don't spill it," Alphonso said.

"I don't think the Acondas even remember why we started fighting in the first place," Wiley said, shaking his head.

Raven had not sat down. He was leaning against the wall by the window.

"Don," he said softly. "Get in positions."

The "positions' had worked quite well last time, Hadley picked up the two skillets she had sat beside her, Robbie picked up the Bible box, and they moved to each side of the door.

Mary Rose picked up a small coal shovel that was laying on the floor and stood next to Hadley. Marge took a position about six feet in front of the door with Geoffrey beside her, ready to pounce like a cat.

"We're backup," Alphonso said as the three men lined up directly behind Marge. Wiley clutched his pillow to his chest.

Wiley Vondra, a man of modern weaponry.

"Give me a minute when he comes in," Marge said. "I want to try out the smoke screen on the cane."

"And Hadley," Mary Rose added, "don't hit him in the nose with that skillet. It's way too messy."

Hadley nodded and raised the skillet ready to strike.

Don walked up to the shed, stopped, and put his ear against the door.

Total quiet.

Even Geoffrey held his breath this time.

"Ron?" Don said softly. "You in there? You in there drinkin' the beer we hid?"

"Beer?" Alphonso said, moving his lips but making no sound.

"Now he tells us," Wiley lip-synced back.

Don waited a minute or two, then he opened the door a crack and looked in.

He saw Marge, Mary Rose and the three men and threw open the door as hard as he could.

Robbie jumped back just in time.

Marge pushed the jewel for a smoke screen.

Nothing.

Hadley wasted no time. She swung the skillet and hit the ugly Aconda squarely in the nose. They could hear it break.

"Oh, really!" Mary Rose said as blood spurted into the air.

Geoffrey made a leap and knocked Don off his feet.

Robbie smashed the Bible box onto his head. Hadley did her skillet trick again.

More rust flew into the air.

Mary Rose began smashing Don Aconda's kneecap with the coal shovel.

Don was younger. And faster.

He put one hand to his head, rolled over and jumped up. He headed straight for Mary Rose.

Marge pushed another jewel.

This one worked. Tripping pellets shot out all over the floor in front of the angry Aconda.

"Damn!" he said as his feet flew into the air and he landed with a thud on his butt.

Hadley swung the skillet full force again. Robbie moved in with the Bible. Mary Rose swung the coal shovel, banged his knee as hard as she could, dislocating it, and Geoffrey did his cat leap and landed squarely on Don Aconda's testicles.

"That's easier than a groin kick," Mary Rose said, holding up the little shovel. "I'm two for two in knee dislocations today."

She looked proud.

Geoffrey straddled the Aconda, two paws on each side, and licked Don's face.

Wiley hurried over and smashed his pillow onto the still-damp face.

"Got two of 'em," he gloated.

Wiley Vondra, two for two in pillow talk.

Raven moved in, took Don by the neck, put his hand on his chest and pressed. Don went limp in his arms.

"Old Apache Trick," he explained, looking at Hadley.

Alphonso picked up the third Aconda and carried him over to his two brothers under the tarp. He limped only a little bit but kept one cane in one hand.

Raven undid the ropes, then retied them.

Hadley retrieved the gag she had torn out for George and handed it to Raven, who stuffed it into Don's mouth.

Wiley picked up the tarp, tossed it up into the air. It spread like wings over the well-tied Acondas and they watched it float gracefully down on top of the three who were seated together like merchandise displayed on a shelf.

"I'll go in and get Con," Raven said. "He should still be out cold. "Then I'll hot wire the truck and get it to a place where I can call the police."

Mary Rose looked at him proudly. "You can hot-wire a truck because you're an Indian."

"No," Raven said. "I can hot-wire a truck because I own a security company."

He chuckled as he went out the door.

"These guys will go up the river for a long time," Wiley said.

"I haven't heard, 'up the river' for years," Marge said. "I do believe that when one door closes and another door opens, it means you're in prison."

"Right," Hadley said. "And when one door closes the hallway to the open door can be very, very long."

Speaking of doors, they heard the door to the house slam.

They saw Con Aconda running full speed toward the truck."

Raven was right behind him.

"He's younger and faster," Wiley said.

"Just wait," Alphonso replied. "Apache Man will think of something. I know, he's hit me enough times."

Raven thought of something.

He stopped, looked at the shed and gave a loud whistle.

Geoffrey's ears went up and he began a monster bound toward the door, which Marge opened just in time.

The big dog had slowed down some, but he was still a menace.

Raven stood solid, pointed to Con, and said, "PLAY!" as loud as he could.

Geoffrey lit up like a Christmas tree.

He was drooling full drool when he took Con down. Con's hand was on the door handle of the driver's side and he didn't let go. Geoffrey heard a bone snap in Con's back and then in his wrist. The door swung fully open just as Geoffrey bounced off, and the heavy door smashed Con with tremendous power into the front fender.

"Ummph!" was the only sound Con made.

He slumped to the ground and Geoffrey, being a quick learner and watching his Indian, jumped on Con's chest and pressed as hard as he could, just as Raven had done in the shed.

Keeping his big paws firmly in place, Geoff looked at Raven and grinned.

Raven grinned back.

Raven picked Con up and threw him, with some effort, over his shoulder. "Not as easy as it used to be," he told the dog. "Do you believe I used to be able to do this with Alphonso's big body?"

Geoffrey believed. He trotted beside Raven with a great look of pride on his ugly, lovable face. His back hurt, his shoulder hurt and every one of his legs ached.

This had been his kind of day.

Raven tied Con up with his brothers.

"A not-so-fearsome foursome," Robbie said, looking at the four of them tied together with Apache knots and gags in their mouths.

Ron had started to come to and was groaning into his gag.

Wiley held the pillow against his face for a few minutes and he quieted down.

"I'm keeping this pillow," Wiley said, looking at the grimy, grey, dirty pillow.

Mary Rose looked at the other girls and gave her head a little, "No he isn't" shake.

Raven smiled, gave Robbie a quick peck on the check and headed for the truck.

"I'll go with you," Wiley yelled, and he followed Raven out the door.

The big truck roared off, its monster wheels crawling over the massive clods and rocks and ruts that made the road impassible for ordinary vehicles.

In just minutes. Raven and Wiley were back. Raven and Alphonso and Wiley drug the four Acondas out onto the lawn.

"We could have done that easier," Marge said to the girls.

The breeze was still gentle, and Hadley noticed how many birds and squirrels had homes in the rows of trees around the old farmhouse.

While they waited, the girls went into the house and used the bathroom. The guys were on their own amongst the trees.

"This had been really nice at one time," Hadley observed as they walked through the kitchen. The old linoleum was grey, and the appliances dated from the 1940's.

"It looks like an ad out of an antique Better Homes and Gardens," Robbie observed.

The kitchen table was an old chrome one and the chairs were missing. No doubt stacked in the shed.

They had just settled back down in those chairs from the shed, when they heard a helicopter.

"I told them they couldn't make it on the road," Raven said. "We've got two choppers coming."

Marge had never lost her wonder at watching a police helicopter land. The first one settled into the spacious back lawn of the house, the other landed in the little field across the road.

"How did you pull off two birds?" Marge asked Raven.

"Used your name in vain," he told her.

An officer approached from each chopper. Each man saw Marge. They all went to her and shook her hand. She smiled; her red cane securely hooked over one arm.

Hadley thought one of the young men wanted to stand at attention and salute Marge.

"If you folks can get across that road, we'll make a couple of trips and take you home," the lead detective said.

"What does he mean, *if we can get across that road?*" Robbie whispered to Hadley. "He should have seen us take down the Acondas."

Hadley smiled and nodded. The skillets had been hung back on their hooks, but Robbie carried the Bible and box like Wiley carried his pillow.

They got across the road.

One of the policemen acted like a kid with a new bike for Christmas when he got to drive

Alphonso's scooter home. He rode it up the field like a veteran, and Hadley, watching from the helicopter window, wondered if he could do a wheelie, he seemed so good.

She squinted hard out the helicopter window. She thought she saw a tiny man, dressed in green, holding onto his top hat with both hands, riding bravely in the bitch seat of the green machine. But Hadley's eyes weren't that great, so she attributed it to the sunlight streaming onto the chopper.

It took two trips to get them all back to Meadow Lakes. Each time they landed on the beautiful grounds, the leaves blowing like the 'before the wild hurricane fly' line in *The Night Before Christmas* poem, faces were at the windows of the retirement community and a small crowd had gathered outside.

As with all things in such a close community, it didn't last long. People there had seen it all.

When the seven friends met that night for dinner, and crowded around table 12, it was as if nothing had happened and that was just what they wanted.

How Much is that Doggie in the Window?
Or Cage?
Or Unheated Shed?

"I can't find him anywhere!" Mary Rose McGill hurried once again across the dining room to grab ahold of table 12, and once again gripped it so hard it made her knuckles white.

"Why don't we get her to come here and sit at the table *first*?" Robbie asked with a smile. "Then she wouldn't be interrupting us with crisis after crisis."

"It is rather getting to be an annoying habit," Hadley added, smiling and winking at Mary Rose, who did not smile or wink back.

"I'm scared half to death," Mary Rose said.

"What happens if you get scared half to death twice?" Robbie grinned.

"OK," Marge said, taking the lead. "Who can't you find?"

"Geoffrey!" Mary Rose said loudly. "Wiley and I have looked all over for him, called him, walked the property and he is nowhere to be found."

"Nowhere to be found," Hadley said. "Sounds like a line from a bad mystery."

"He's probably just in someone's apartment," Marge added. "How long has he been gone?"

"Since six this morning," Mary Rose said. "He was there when I got up to go to the bathroom at five o'clock. Then I woke up again at six, and he was gone."

"Holy Moly, it's noon now," Robbie said.

"He may have fallen asleep in someone's apartment, then they left and didn't notice him, so he's stuck until they come home," Hadley said hopefully.

"He would have barked if he'd been alone in someone else's apartment and someone in the hall or next door would have heard him." Marge looked around at the girls. "Call Wiley, Mary Rose. Tell him to come on down for lunch and after we eat, we'll all go looking for the Prince of Paws.

"We'll find him."

Mary Rose called Wiley.

Wiley came, as did Alphonso and Raven, which is more than they could say for Geoffrey.

Lunch was quieter than usual. Mary Rose and Wiley updated the others on their search for the big dog, which had been so thorough it was boring.

"We even walked down to the empty bar that used to be in the next block," Wiley said, looking at Alphonso. "Remember how we used to go there when you first moved in?"

Alphonso laughed. "I remember how we wanted some excitement and tried to rob the place."

Wiley grinned.

"Problem was," Alphonso went on, addressing the others, "the bartender recognized us right off and instead of giving us the money from the cash register, she poured us two beers."

Wiley laughed.

"What was her name?" he asked. "I don't remember."

"Modesty," Marge answered. "Modesty Lium, like in Mausoleum, so we called her Mausi Lium. She worked for that funeral director, Morgan Graves."

"The bar was Viva La Crypt," Hadley put in.

And the vampire who lived at the funeral home was named, Sam," Marge added.

"How did a common name like Sam get in there for a vampire?" Robbie grinned. "Couldn't he be like Phyllis Diller's husband and be called, 'Fang'?"

Mary Rose was quiet, still looking worried.

"OK," Robbie went on, "I'll volunteer the name of the funeral home. Remember it? Billow deGround." She shook her head. "I'm still wondering how a vampire named Sam got into that mess.'"

"He was a very sweet vampire," Mary Rose added, finally paying attention to what was going on.

"I miss that bar," Alphonso said.

Wiley nodded.

They were quiet.

"Do you want to cover all that ground again to find Geoffrey?" Marge asked.

Mary Rose nodded. "I have to find him. He's old and he's seemed so tired lately." She paused and took a deep breath. "I'm afraid he's gone away to die, like animals do."

They looked at her.

Hadley reached out and took ahold of Mary Rose's hand.

"I don't want him to die," Mary Rose said softly. "But if that's what he's going to do, I don't want him to die alone."

As if they were one person, they rose from the table to go find Geoffrey.

"First stop," Alphonso said as he motored the green machine down the hall, "is to do a master call."

There was a button on the phone in his office that, once pushed, allowed Alphonso or Sheryl to send a message to every telephone in every apartment at Meadow Lakes. It was great for announcements and emergencies – such as, "the water to the entire building will be turned off immediately due to a leak." It could be both exciting and frustrating at the same time. Soaped-up people in their showers had never gotten over that one.

They gathered around Alphonso's desk.

Alphonso pushed the button.

"Residents, this is Alphonso Greatwood. We are unable to find Geoffrey the Mastiff. You all know Geoffrey, and if he is enjoying a good nap in your apartment and not wanting to leave, would you tell him Mary Rose is worried and bring him to the office right away? Thank you."

They waited.

After about fifteen minutes, they heard footsteps in the short hall leading to Alphonso's office.

Zed Zucker stuck his homely head through the open door.

"Dog took a run for it, eh Greatwood?" He grinned a mean grin at Alphonso. "Old dude for a big dog. Probably went off somewhere to lay down and croak. Might look in the chicken yard."

Mary Rose gasped and put her hand over her mouth.

She had thought of that and looked in the chicken yard. Meadow Lakes had, for years, kept exotic chickens in a neat, penned area on the property. Zed Zonker had not liked them since he had been treed two years ago by the alpha rooster.

Wiley Vondra stood up; fists clenched.

"Didn't come here to talk about dumb dogs," Zed continued. He took a step toward Alphonso and stared up at him. "I saw that Leprechaun again. He was climbing through a window in the basement of the storage shed."

They all looked at each other. The community had an attractive, large storage shed with a full basement underneath it.

Mary Rose and Wiley had checked the shed, but they hadn't checked the windows to the shed's basement.

"Take care of it, Greatwood. Oh, and Vondra, speaking of Leprechauns and your family's intelligence, did you hear about the Mother Superior who was in the convent and there was a knock on the door? She opened it and there were two Leprechauns, hats in their hands. 'Mother Superior,' one of them says, 'do you have any Leprechaun nuns in this convent?'

'No, my son, we don't have any Leprechaun nuns in this convent.'

'So Mother, do you know of any Leprechaun nuns in all of Ireland?'

Mother Superior thinks for a minute and says, 'No, I don't think there are any Leprechaun nuns in all of Ireland.'

The one Leprechaun turns to the other and slaps him on the back. 'See ya old fool. Like I told ya. You've been dating a penguin.'"

Before anyone could say anything, Zed turned toward Alphonso.

"And Greatwood, what do the Kansas City Chiefs and a possum have in common?"

He chuckled and before Alphonso could say anything, Zed almost yelled, "They both play dead at home and get killed on the road!!"

He looked at Raven, who was standing by the window, his arms folded, staring at Zed. "I had a dumb Indian joke," he gloated, "but I forgot it just like I forget all dumb Indians."

Again, before anyone could say anything, Zed Zonker was out the door. They could hear him laughing all the way down the hall.

"What did you say earlier about loving him?" Alphonso asked Hadley.

"If I said it, I didn't mean it," she answered. "Zed Zonker should check himself into the Hokey Pokey clinic and turn himself around."

They all headed toward the door.

"Leprechauns aren't in season this time of year, are they?" Mary Rose asked Wiley.

"No. But we'll hunt one anyway," he grinned. The storage shed was on the agenda, Leprechaun or not.

"Son of a gun!" Alphonso said. They were standing by the storage shed, and he was leaning forward on his canes, staring through an open window whose glass had been carefully removed. The window was leaning neatly up against the wall beside the opening and was so carefully placed it was almost impossible to notice it.

"Geoffrey!" Mary Rose called a little too loudly, aiming her voice at the open window.

Silence.

Then from inside the shed's basement came a soft, almost impossible to hear, whine, like a baby's mewling.

"That was a whine," Robbie said.

"It was a tiny cry alright," Hadley said.

"I've got the keys," Alphonso said.

They went to the front of the shed and Alphonso opened the door with a key that hung with many others from a jailer's keyring that had gone through more than one pocket on more than one pair of pants.

All was quiet inside.

The shed was neat and clean, filled with yard equipment and planting supplies. Immediately to the right of the door was a staircase with eight steps leading to the full basement.

Raven started down, followed by the others.

Alphonso was last, and ever the athlete, he threw his canes down ahead of him, grabbed hold of the handrails on each side of the steps, stuck his legs straight out and slid to the bottom.

It was impressive.

"You should wear gloves for that," Wiley said.

Alphonso nodded and rubbed his hands.

In one corner, away from the draft that came in through the removed window and out of sight from anyone casually passing by, was a large plastic bin. The top had been removed and laid to one side. The big bin had been fitted with two or three blankets and sitting beside it was a dog dish full of clean water and a dog food bowl half filled with fresh kibbles.

"I don't think Geoffrey did all this by himself," Hadley said, looking at the bin, blankets and bowls.

They nodded; then sad smiles came across their faces.

Raising her head above the rim of the plastic bin was a sorrowful-looking little dog.

They moved closer.

"She's a little cocker," Robbie said.

"No," Hadley said, "she's a little skeleton."

The dog's bones could be seen under her matted, mangy skin. Her hair was falling out in places, her eyes were running with yellow mucus and one of her paws had obviously been viciously torn and had healed badly.

Squirming and squealing softly beside her were four beautiful little golden cocker spaniel puppies, newborns, not more than several days old. Momma flinched as she looked at the visitors, afraid they would hurt her, but after watching them for just a minute, she rolled over onto her side so her babies could nurse.

"She's got milk," Mary Rose said.

They stood in silence watching her, keeping a safe distance so she wouldn't be spooked.

All at once they could hear footsteps outside the shed and Geoffrey lumbered through the open window. He landed awkwardly on all fours, looked up and saw his people.

His eyes went stupidly wide.

His ears flew into the air.

His tail reacted like a flagpole and went straight up.

His mouth dropped open and when that happened, the tiny cocker puppy he was carrying fell to the floor with a soft flop.

Hadley grabbed the baby and held it to her heart. It was a little wet from Geoffrey's mouth, and it was also soft and sweet and had that beautiful new puppy smell.

Mary Rose grabbed Geoffrey and held him to her heart as well.

In just a second a pair of green legs and a green rear end slid in backward through the window. "That's the last one, Geoff," a high-pitched voice said. "We got all five of 'em."

As they stared at him, a tiny green Leprechaun landed square on the basement floor and turned, still holding onto his top hat. The buckles on his boots shone in the sun coming in through the window.

He saw them all and his eyes and mouth mimicked Geoffrey's. If he had a tail, it would have been a flagpole, too.

"Uh Oh," he said, backing up against the wall. They looked at him.

He looked back.

Hadley squinted and took a step forward, then she looked at both Robbie and Mary Rose who were staring, open-mouthed, at the little man in green. The three women had all taken a step closer and were bent over to better see his face.

"Clyde?" they said together.

"Ladies," the little man answered.

There was just a second's hesitation, then all three – Hadley, Robbie and Mary Rose – dived onto the little man with the top hat and bright buckles. Wiley took one step forward, grinned from ear to ear and stayed in the close background, watching the women smother a midget.

There were squeals and laughs and tears and hugs and the wonderful craziness that comes when you see someone you love who has been gone for years.

Marge, Alphonso and Raven took one step backward, lined up side-by-side and looked at each other. Geoffrey, who had that doggie sense that he had been caught doing a Bad Dog thing, slipped quietly behind Raven and peeked his ugly head out from around the Indian's leg.

"Where have you been!?"

"Have you heard from the others?"

"How did you get here?"

And the one that quieted them: "What in the world are you doing being a Leprechaun?" It was Mary Rose who asked.

Silence with a few gasps for breaths.

"I just always wanted to be a Leprechaun," the little man said with a grin. "I spent six months in Ireland in a study program on Irish myths, and I fell in love with them. They have wonderful powers and they can cause all kinds of trouble."

He looked at them, one-by-one, his eyes twinkling.

"And that's me," he said with a cheery smile.

Alphonso leaned toward Raven. "He's a friggin' midget!"

"Either that or a Denver Bronco's receiver after you landed on him," Raven said with a small smile.

Marge overheard both statements and nodded. Geoffrey ducked back behind his Indian. He stood straight and looked around Raven's leg. He was a perfect picture of a dog who was thigh-high to an Apache.

Wiley stepped forward, clapped him on the back and shook the little man's hand.

"OK," Marge said. "You got our attention. Who is he?" She looked at the midget. "Who are you and don't say you have an Irish name."

The little man turned toward her. Hadley was holding one of his hands and Robbie the other. It looked as if they were going to lift him into the air and swing him back and forth like parents do when their three-year-old walks between them holding their hands.

The little man let go of the two BOOB Girls and moved toward Marge, Alphonso and Raven.

"No Irish name, but it will still surprise you. I'm Clyde Goldberg."

"A Jewish midget?" Marge asked.

"A Jewish Leprechaun?" Alphonso asked.

Raven said, "Hmmm."

"Hey," Clyde joked, pointing at Raven. "Your name is Five Horns and yours," he said to

Alphonso, "is Greatwood. The Great Wood himself. And from what I hear," he looked at Marge and smiled a sweet smile. "You are Marge Aaron and when you introduced yourself you told these nice ladies that if they said it fast it sounded like 'margarine.' So, you'd 'butter be good.'"

He moved directly in front of the trio and held out his hand. "And the best name of all," he said, pointing to the three ladies behind him, is. 'The BOOB Girls.'" They all shook hands.

"He does good research," Robbie said.

Hadley stepped forward. "Ten years ago, Clyde and his brothers lived here with their aunt, Evangeline Goldberg." She looked around at Robbie and Mary Rose. "Evangeline made the best cinnamon rolls in the world!"

They nodded.

"She also gave us The Four Great Religious Truths," Robbie grinned.

Mary Rose and Hadley both giggled.

Robbie had not let go of Clyde's left hand.

"The four great religious truths," she continued. "One," and she raised one finger. "Palestinians do not recognize Jewish rights to the Holy Land. Two," another finger joined the first, "Jews do not recognize Jesus as their Messiah." She looked at Clyde and grinned. He grinned back. "Three," another finger, "Protestants do not recognize the Pope as their religious leader, and four," she looked at Clyde again. "Four: Baptists do not recognize each other at Hooters."

Hadley, Mary Rose, Robbie and Clyde laughed.

Marge, Alphonso and Raven looked stunned.

"What's more," Hadley added. "There were four brothers: Robert, Reuben, Leonard and Clyde. They were known as 'The BOOB Boys.'" She looked at Robbie and Mary Rose.

"The Burned Out Old Bastards." Clyde joined them as the three said it together.

The others continued to look stunned; all except Geoffrey who had decided the excitement was more than he could take. He walked to the big bin that held the dogs, crawled in and curled up next to the mother, who licked his nose and kept her eyes on his people. Geoffrey took up all the room available. The puppies snuggled tight up against their mother.

"Robert was a minister who always wore a suit," Hadley explained. "He had a Bible in the suit pocket that saved his life when Clyde accidentally shot him while we were robbing a grave."

Marge's eyebrows had a conversation with her hairline. "Robbing a grave?"

"Doesn't matter," Mary Rose replied. "It was the wrong grave."

No one said anything more about the grave.

"Rueben was a huge construction guy with a chartreuse van," Hadley continued.

"We were with him when he died of pneumonia," Mary Rose added.

She, Hadley, Robbie and Clyde nodded soberly.

"Leonard was a dear. And he never spoke a word because of aliens," Hadley said, and she looked at Robbie.

"He always wore white – everything white – and he had a beautiful tin foil hat with a point on top. It kept him from being kidnapped by aliens." Mary Rose looked as if she loved this story. "He ran off with our new BOOB Girl, Calamity Doodles, and joined the circus."

Mary Rose said this as if half the population ended up joining the circus.

"Then there was me," Clyde said proudly. "A Leprechaun!"

He got hugs again all the way around from the three women standing with him.

There's a Lot of Evil in the World

Raven interrupted the energetic reunion by simply pointing to the dog and puppies and saying, "How?"

"Is he talking Tonto Talk or asking a question?" Mary Rose asked Robbie.

"Definitely a question," Robbie answered.

"Oh, that - - them - -," Clyde stammered. "That is a little project of Geoffrey's and mine."

Geoffrey heard his name and the touch of anxiety in Clyde's voice, climbed out of the bin and moved close to hide behind Raven.

They all looked at Clyde except Geoffrey, who lay down and put his paws over his eyes.

"When I first came here, I just wanted to see how long it would take for someone to find me. I played Leprechaun for a good long while."

"Wait a minute," Raven said. "You followed us to the farmhouse and opened the window in the bedroom where they were keeping Wiley!"

"Yep. I'm an expert at getting through basement windows. I crawled in while you were on the other side of the house, slipped past the passed-out dude, opened the window then hid in another bedroom."

"I DID see you on the back of Alphonso's scooter coming back from the farmhouse," Hadley said.

"Yep," Clyde said.

"Dogs," Raven reminded him.

"I was here, and I lived in secret in one of the guest rooms. I still have Aunt Evangeline's key fob, so I could move around the place pretty easily."

He looked at Alphonso. "That guest room on three could really use a new toilet. The one in there stops up with nothing in it."

Alphonso nodded. "I'll make a note."

"I was getting out of the shower one day, and when I pulled back the shower curtain, I was face-to-face with that." He looked around for Geoffrey, saw him behind Raven, and pointed to the big, ugly face.

"And I do mean face-to-face," Clyde smiled. "That is one big puppy."

Geoffrey was playing it safe. He kept his paws over his eyes.

"You were always a dog whisperer," Hadley smiled.

"Yep, and this one began to lick my face and snuggle up until we both ended up flat in the shower. He smelled like it was time to be groomed, so I gave him a shower and a good scrub, and he loved it."

"I thought he was lasting a long while between washes," Mary Rose said to Wiley.

"Dogs," Raven said again, pointing to the plastic bin. All the puppies were full and sound asleep. Momma was watching the humans with one eye and Geoffrey with the other.

"I was doing some field research," Clyde said.

"Field research?" Robbie asked, her eyebrows raising.

"Looking for a field," Clyde said. "I have this big pot of gold." He looked around. "Well, not real gold, but those good chocolates that are wrapped to look like gold coins." He took a breath. "And I wanted to put the pot of gold in the middle of a field, then use some state-of-the-art special effects with my computer to create a rainbow coming out of the pot."

"OK," Marge said, speaking up for the first time, "you wanted to be the Leprechaun with a pot of gold and dance around it and invite someone to catch you, like the old myth says, and you'll dump the chocolate on their head."

"Well said," Clyde replied. "So Big Dog here," he pointed to Geoffrey, who had lifted one paw off one eye and was listening intently, ears high in the air, "and I wandered around looking for a field and we came across a large spot of pure evil."

"Are you talking about New Age stuff where you feel evil energy in the field, like Vortexes or things like that?" Mary Rose asked.

"No," Clyde said. "And I understand Vortexes have good energy. No, this was a very evil place." He looked at them.

Geoffrey slid the other paw off his eye.

"We found a puppy mill," Clyde said. His voice had a slight dramatic tone to it. Everyone could see that this was very important to him; more so when Geoffrey pulled himself up and limped over to stand beside Clyde.

It looked as if the midget's horse had just arrived. Clyde put his arm over Geoff's shoulders.

"We went back when it got dark, and we heard this lady," he pointed to Mama Dog, "groaning and whining. We unfastened the gate, slipped in and saw her in a pile of straw with tiny babies. There was no one around and you would not believe all the garbage and filth that surrounded her." He shook his head. "No food. No water."

They looked again at the skeletal, dirty little dog lying in the bin, cuddled closely by soft puppies.

"Both Geoff and I knew what we had to do. I picked her up and I carried her back here while Geoffrey carried a puppy in his mouth. We left her and went back, but we had to wait a while because lights started coming on in the house and around the cages."

"Cages?" Hadley asked.

"Stacked five high and filled with dogs," Clyde said. "The dogs were so beaten down that only a couple of them gave wimpy little barks when we came in."

"We sneaked in and made another trip, but I could only take two puppies and Geoffrey one, so we went back for the last one." He pointed to the bin. "And that's the one who dropped in on you."

"You haven't slept all night," Mary Rose said, rubbing Clyde's back.

"Nope. And we've got to do something. We've got to take that place down. Those dogs in the cages are in terrible shape." He yawned.

"You and Geoffrey head up to the guest room," Alphonso said, taking control. "Get some sleep." He looked at Robbie. "We'll do our own field research on that puppy mill."

Clyde bent down and rubbed Mama Dog's head. Geoffrey licked her face, then licked one of the puppies.

Hadley leaned forward to pat Mama Dog as well. The little cocker flinched, but Hadley gave her a gentle rub and pat. "I don't think she's ever been bathed."

"Remember Edith Ann?" Robbie put in. Mary Rose and Hadley nodded. Edith Ann was a sweet little dog who had been bred out in a puppy mill when they went full-time RVing in 2009. She had been turned loose, then used for target practice. Taking Edith Ann, who had become the fifth BOOB Girl to the vet, was when they first heard about the cruelty of what, in some places, is registered as *Dog Farming*.

"We need to get Mama Dog to a vet, too," Hadley observed.

"We use Dr. Pete," Mary Rose said. "He has a mobile veterinarian van and makes house calls." She was already puling her cell phone out of her pocket to dial Dr. Pete, the House Call Vet.

"In the meantime," Robbie said, reaching for Raven's hand and moving toward the stairs leading up to the door of the shed. "let's do that field research we talked about." She looked back at the others. "Meet us at my computer."

"I'll put the window back in place," Wiley said, heading for the stairs. He stooped to rub Mama Dog's head on the way over.

There was a ray of sun streaming in through the window of the shed and washing Mama Dog in its soft light. As they left, she snuggled her babies closer to her, lay her head down and went to sleep.

The Ten Mule-Team Lorax

A mule is an animal with long funny ears
Kicks up at anything he hears
His back is brawny, but his brain is weak
He's just plain stupid with a stubborn streak
And by the way, if you hate to go to school
You may grow up to be a mule

Swinging on A Star (Bing Crosby)

"Unless someone like you cares a whole awful lot,
Nothing is going to get better. It's not."

Dr. Seuss, The Lorax

Hadley was standing in Robbie's bathroom, looking into the mirror. "Time may be a great healer," she said out loud, "but it's a lousy beautician."

She washed her hands, straightened her hair, and headed for the door.

"I'm next," Mary Rose said, standing just outside the bathroom.

Robbie's bathroom was decorated with South African artwork, statuettes and tasteful pictures. The rugs were beautiful. All the girls, and even Alphonso, made a point to make a trip there every time they were in her apartment.

Hanging over the toilet was a little sign Hadley had given her. "If you're waiting for a sign, this is it." Hadley always smiled no matter how often she read it.

It was early afternoon when they finally gathered around Robbie's computer. Alphonso had gone to his apartment and returned with two bottles of wine. Marge had grabbed some cheese and crackers.

"Now, when I think about drinking responsibly, that means I try not to spill it," Alphonso chuckled as he poured four glasses of Chardonnay and watched Wiley Vondra come through the door with a six-pack of beer. That, "not spilling it," was becoming his favorite statement/joke and it was beginning to earn eye rolls.

Robbie was at the table typing rapid little strokes into her computer. The others had dragged chairs and gathered around her except for Clyde who, literally, climbed onto a bar stool for a better perch, and Geoffrey, who squeezed between feet beneath the table.

"Oh, Sweet Jesus," Robbie said.

The others were quiet.

She read aloud into a hushed silence.
"Here's what it says about puppy mills:
- Usually unkept, sometimes filthy environments
- Dogs live in cages stacked sometimes, five high
- Frequently paws never touch the ground
- Feet slip through the cage floor and cause serious injury
- Dogs are usually not vaccinated or not vaccinated thoroughly
- Food comes from the floors of dog food factories
- Clean water often given only twice a week, sometimes coming only when it rains
- Seldom if ever bathed since only the puppies are viewed.
- Cages, with dogs inside, are hosed down top to bottom to wash cage and dogs
- Visitors are never allowed to see inside the dog enclosure

- Dogs kept indoors are in unheated buildings, with stacked cages
- Most are in violation of state laws
- Dogs are never given names or socialized (petted, talked to, etc.)
- Customers who inquire about a puppy are usually met in a parking lot at a Walmart, Target, or other shopping center
- When named, property names are inviting such as "Fido Farm" or "Puppy Ranch"
- Sick puppies are frequently sold
- Dogs are bred out, breeding in every cycle

"Do you want me to go on?" Robbie asked.

They stared at her.

She typed some more.

"Ah. I found the puppy mill from which Clyde and Geoffrey rescued Mama Dog. It was listed under, 'Nebraska's 100 Worst Puppy Mills.'"

She read off fine after fine, violation after violation, report after report of complaints that puppies had found a home then died shortly after being purchased.

"We have to do something!" Mary Rose said. Tears were forming in her eyes, and she rubbed her foot over Geoffrey's side as he lay sleeping at her feet.

"Looks like everything that's legal has already been done, and they're still going strong," Marge said, twisting her cane in her hands.

"You want to do something illegal?" Raven asked. He stood up, went to the kitchen counter, folded his arms and stood beside Clyde perched on his barstool.

They looked at him.

There was more silence.

They looked at Marge.

She looked back. "I've never been arrested," she said, sounding hopeful.

"Then it's time for some adventure," Wiley added, as if being kidnapped hadn't been adventure enough.

"Meadow Lakes will post bail," Alphonso said, his voice sounding reassuring. "I'll leave a note for

Sheryl in case I'm behind bars, too." He grinned at Raven. "A lot of the hits you did on me when we played football were illegal."

Raven grinned back.

"Might be good publicity," Alphonso added.

Hadley looked surprised. "Illegal? Just what the hell are you thinking about?" she said loudly.

"Destroying the place," Raven said, a mischievious smile still on his face.

"Talk on," Marge said to him.

"I have a client about twenty miles outside of Omaha. He raises mules."

"Mules?" Mary Rose asked.

"A mule is an offspring of a male donkey and a female horse, usually a draft or working horse," Robbie informed her.

"I know that," Mary Rose said.

"Because of the strength of the draft horse, if you breed her with a big, strong donkey you have one powerful animal," Robbie went on.

"With long funny ears," Wiley winked at her.

"I know that," Mary Rose said.

"When we were growing up, remember the ads with 'Twenty Mule-team Borax?'" Hadley grinned.

"I know that, too," Mary Rose said again.

"My client, Muley, has what he calls a 'Ten Mule-Team Lorax,'" Raven said. He looked at Mary Rose.

"I didn't know that," she said.

"A Lorax is a mythical old man who champions nature and the environment," Robbie noted. "Remember Dr. Seuss and his book, The Lorax? 'I am the Lorax. I speak for the trees.'"

They nodded.

"Right," Raven said. "Muley is an environmental nut. He recycles what he's already recycled. He says his mule team speaks for the land. They fertilize it, aureate it with their hoofs and graze it pure."

"They're infertile, too, aren't they?" Hadley asked.

"Yes!" Mary Rose said.

She knew that, too.

"They don't have children because they would make half-assed parents," Mary Rose gleamed.

They all looked at her.

Then they all laughed.

Mary Rose laughed the hardest.

Geoffrey farted, yawned and went back to sleep.

"What do mules have to do with closing down a puppy mill?" Alphonso asked.

"They're trained mules," Raven answered. "Muley can have them pull his big wagon, they can tear down wherever the dogs are, and do whatever Muley wants." He looked at Clyde.

"Where are the dogs on the property?" He asked.

"In a big shed about half the size of a barn," Clyde said.

Raven nodded. "They tear down the shed, we load the puppies into the wagon and take them to a no-kill shelter."

"I know where one is," Mary Rose chimed in, excitement in her voice. "It's south of here and it's great. 'Protecting Paws.'"

"You think the six of us can lift dogs in cages into a wagon?" Wiley asked Raven. "Get a life, son."

He took a long drag on his beer.

"That's why we have Muley," Raven said.

"We need to get the owners out of there," Marge said. She hesitated, looked around, then broke into a grin. "Leave that to me. I'll get them taken in for questioning. That way, they'll be off the property."

"On what charge?" Hadley asked.

"How about grand theft?" Marge grinned. "I've always liked the sound of that. The words are like music." She whispered them to herself. "*Grand Theft.*"

"She can do that," Mary Rose whispered to Wiley. Wiley nodded.

"All I have to do is make a phone call." Marge was still grinning as she pulled out her phone.

"I'll alert the shelter that they have puppies coming," Mary Rose said. She was so excited she bounced up and down a couple of times.

They all, including Clyde, gathered around the table and began to make wicked, illegal and righteous plans to destroy a little pocket of cruelty.

Take it down!

Marge made a phone call.

Raven made a phone call.

Mary Rose made a phone call.

They consulted with each other.

They all got out their calendars and marked a day two days ahead.

Mary Rose and Geoffrey took a walk.

Wiley, Alphonso, Raven and Clyde had another beer.

Hadley took a nap.

Robbie poured herself a cup of coffee and went back to her computer to study puppy mills.

The next day was perfectly normal. Clyde disappeared to do what he thought would be his last day as a Leprechaun. He wanted to shadow Zed Zonker, showing up in the corner of Zed's eye, then vanishing. It promised to be a productive day.

Mary Rose sat for awhile at her computer and studied mules. They were fascinating.

"Listen to this, Wiley," she said excitedly. "Mules date back to at least 6000 BC and they were royal animals. Get this, King David used mules to create a parade bearing lavish feasts for his inauguration. His son, Solomon, road to the celebration on a hinny." She paused. "I always thought a hinny was a rear end, but it's a cross between a male horse and female donkey."

She thought for a few seconds.

"You could say King Solomon rode to his father's inauguration on his father's hinny." She giggled and put her hand over her mouth.

Wiley said, "Ummhhh".

A small, "Ummhhh" would not stop Mary Rose McGill. "King David himself had a royal mule he rode. In Egypt, mules pulled chariots. A favorite royal mule was sometimes killed and buried in a pyramid with a pharaoh."

She took a dep breath and went on reading. "In Mesopotamia, the story was told that the King was reprimanded and asked to 'Please use a mule instead of the common horse', as his royal position demanded.

"People of ancient Ethiopia gave the mule the highest status of all the animals. The mule was highly valued in ancient Greece as a pack animal and to draw carriages. Mules had much harder hooves than horses and were better suited to cover the rocky terrain found in Greece. Also, the mule was easier to train than the horse, and could cover a 50-mile area in a day and need only four or five hours of sleep."

She paused, put her hands in her lap and said, "Can you imagine just needing four or five hours of sleep? It sounds like us old people at night."

Wiley Vondra was sound asleep himself, his head laid back in his recliner.

"Hannibal," Mary Rose read, "the young man who crossed the alps – he had mules with him as well as elephants, and they think he probably road a mule across the mountains. I think that is just amazing."

She did a couple of clicks on links on the computer page.

"Now, the mule is the symbol of Missouri. We are 'stubborn as a mule,' but this says they are easier to train than horses. Well, Bing Crosby can sing about, 'their back is brawny, but their brain is weak. They're just plain stupid with a stubborn streak,' but that's not true. I think mules are tremendous animals. I wish I'd had one growing up. You were a cowboy, Wiley, did you ever ride a mule?"

Wiley's nose twitched, he gave a soft snore and slept on.

Go Big Red!

It was a cloudy, dismal day, a perfect day to destroy something malicious.

They waited in Alphonso's van, Clyde standing at the very front so he could see out the windshield. The van was backed into a grove of trees several yards from the puppy mill with a clear view of the house and the big shed where the dogs were housed.

The police car had been in front of the house for several minutes.

"Ought to be coming out about now," Marge said, glancing at the time on her phone.

Almost before she finished speaking, the door to the house opened. Two detectives exited, followed by a couple with their hands behind their backs and in handcuffs. A third officer was close behind them. His hand barely touching the man's back.

"Whoa," Marge said. "Perp walk. Good job." She chuckled a soft chuckle. "See the cop getting in behind the wheel? That's Ryan. When he was a recruit and brand new on the force, I was one of his instructors. We were doing scenarios of 'What would you do?' and the scenario was, 'If you had to arrest your own mother, what would you do?' And Ryan seriously said, 'Call for backup!'"

Robbie and Alphonso laughed.

"Did you do the Grand Theft thing?" Hadley asked.

"No, couldn't think of anything that sounded logical, so I went with cruelty to animals. They'll show the police all their licenses and permits and stuff and be fined and released, but my guys can make it last for two, maybe three hours." She thought for a minute. "Four hours if they're having a good day."

The couple was loaded into the back seat of the unmarked car, the detectives putting a hand on their heads as they got in. They were an unusually thin couple, dressed in jeans and work shirts and what looked to Marge to be Doc Martin boots.

The detectives drove off.

Alphonso moved the van into the driveway of the puppy mill, driving it in as far as possible.

They waited just a few minutes until they saw a magnificent wagon, pulled by ten gigantic mules pull up beside them. The wagon was shaped like a long, elegant stagecoach, obviously designed to give rides. The red, yellow and black colors gleamed spotlessly. The big wheels were bright yellow, the wagon itself was red trimmed in black with enough chrome to blind a squirrel.

Driving the wagon was a large man, almost as big as Alphonso, and sitting beside him was another man of equal size. They had well-groomed white beards and each head was topped with a shock of gleaming white hair. Both men were dressed in black pants, black shirts and black boots. Each had a matching black hat resting on his knees. Robbie's eyes got wide, Hadley's eyebrows went up, Marge drew in a deep breath and said, "Wow," and Mary Rose McGill nearly shrieked with delight at the sight.

Hadley thought it was as if thee circus had just come to town.

"Muley," Raven said, pointing to the wagon.

Alphonso and Wiley nodded. They all climbed out of the van and Mary Rose scurried to the wagon and looked up at the driver.

"I'm Mary Rose McGill and I know about mules," she said breathlessly. She began to shoot out facts like a BB gun in the hands of a twelve-year-old. Muley looked amused and pleased.

He hopped down to be with Mary Rose, and not missing a beat, took her by the hand and led her to the lead mule.

The mules were gorgeous. They were huge, their pointed ears held high and proud. Their eyes were bright, and their coats were a beautiful mixture of browns and blacks.

The driver turned to Mary Rose as they stood beside the big animal. "I'm Muley," he said. "This is Washington." Still holding Mary Rose's hand, he placed it gently on the mule's strong neck.

Mary Rose gasped and laid her head on the soft hair on the big shoulder.

Robbie looked at Hadley. "You hear all those facts she had about mules?"

Hadley nodded.

"I hate it when she's smarter than I am."

Hadley smiled. "You hate it when anybody's smarter than you."

They all gathered around the massive and very impressive team.

The man riding shotgun with Muley walked up and stood beside Alphonso. They were nearly the same size and like Muley, this gentleman had a trim white beard and looked good in black denim, cowboy boots and the Stetson hat, which he still held in his hands.

"This is Stooge," Muley said. "He's my brother. Same mother. Same Father."

Hadley looked at Robbie. "Muley? Stooge? Funny names?"

Robbie shook her head. "Somehow it fits," she said. "But I'll say it if you want it," She took a breath. "Sweet Jesus!"

They smiled at each other and turned back toward Muley and Stooge. Mary Rose was gently rubbing Washington's neck.

"He's named after George Washington, and he's my lead mule," Muley said. "George Washington, father of our country, was the first known mule breeder in the country. He was a champion Muleteer."

Mary Rose raised her eyebrows.

"Muleteer," Muley repeated. They all moved closer to hear him.

"First used as an active word in 1587 in Europe. It means someone who drives the mules. Also known in this country as a 'Mule Skinner."

He smiled and looked around. "We don't skin mules," he chuckled. He reached a hand toward Stooge and the other big man slapped a long, rather thick whip into it. The whip was wrapped in a tight circle and could fasten onto a belt.

"If they argue with us, and believe me, they do, we snap them lightly on the skin with this special whip. We 'skin' 'em a little or tickle their skin." He looked around at them. "It doesn't hurt. Only an idiot would abuse a mule."

He was loving his role as teacher. So was Robbie, who had steadily moved closer. Raven was leaning casually against the wagon, smiling at Robbie's enthusiasm.

"Allow me to introduce you before we get to work," Muley said. He began to point at each magnificent animal, whose coats were gleaming in the sun.

"You've met Washington. Next to him is Hamilton. The two behind them are John Adams and Quincy Adams."

He laid a gentle hand on the next mule. "This is Burr and next to her is Jackson."

He took a step back and rubbed the neck of the seventh animal. "This sweet lady is Jefferson," he said. The mule snorted. "She never liked that name." He grinned.

"She does like teaming up with Hancock, here," he said, pointing to the mule next to Jefferson.

He moved to the two mules closest to the wagon. "And last but by no means least, let me present Franklin and Monroe."

"They're all named after famous Americans of history," Robbie smiled.

"Indeed, my dear," Muley said. "And almost all of those named bred mules. These are the greatest animals in history, I believe."

"I agree!" Mary Rose exclaimed.

Marge grinned. "I was actually hoping you were going to tell us their names were Dasher, Dancer, Prancer and Vixen."

Hadley joined her, "On Comet, on Cupid, on Donner and Blitzen."

They laughed.

"Time to work," Raven said.

Muley unhitched the two lead mules, Washington and Hamilton.

Stooge led them away from the wagon toward the big shed where the dogs were kept captive.

With very little effort, Muley directed the mules to turn around. Their rears faced the shed. Both mules watched him with interest. He moved forward and talked to them as if he were giving them instructions. Then he turned their heads toward Stooge, who was holding a boom box.

The group had been so intent on watching Washington and Hamilton that they hadn't noticed Stooge going back to the wagon to get the big CD player.

Stooge pressed a button.

There was a loud drum roll.

Then the University of Nebraska marching band blared out with the Nebraska fight song.

"Go Huskers!" Marge yelled.

"Go Chiefs!" Alphonso yelled.

"Go mules," Raven said under his breath.

At exactly the same time, Washington and Hamilton shot their hind legs into the air and kicked the shed door as hard as they could.

Wood cracked.

A shattering sound filled the air.

Dust flew.

Wiley saw three dead bolts shoot high into the sky.

"Go Big Red!" Muley and Stooge yelled together.

The mules kicked again, in time with the music. The shattering sound came again.

"That is one spectacular kick," Robbie said. She had moved over near Raven. She wrapped her sweater, which had *Creighton Blue Jays* on the back, around her shoulders and thought how cool and brisk the day was. "Great football weather, or mule kicking weather," she said loud enough to be heard over the fight song. She looked at Raven. "Go Big Red!"

He nodded, touched her hand and began to move toward the shed which was now partially collapsed.

Stooge took the two mules, led them around to face the collapsed front of the shed, then went inside. Wiley and Raven followed.

They were only gone a few minutes. They came back with a cage in each hand. Dogs in the cages were cowering and shaking. The girls could see the pitiful shaking from where they were standing.

Stooge produced large leather straps and fastened two cages securely to each side of the mules. He turned them and they came back to the wagon with eight cages, a dog in each cage.

He deftly lifted the cages into the wagon.

"We can do that," Marge said, and she and Alphonso moved to stand beside Stooge.

He went back for eight more cages while Muley unhitched the next pair of mules.

It was a strange yet exciting vision to watch ten mules line up, carry eight cages each to the wagon and watch everyone there lifting cages and breathing hard.

Clyde helped by getting under the cages and pushing from beneath as they were hoisted into the wagon.

"I am going to be so stiff tomorrow," Hadley announced.

They all nodded.

In less than an hour they were finished.

The dogs were safely in the wagon, which could not possibly hold one more cage. There had been a few barks and yips, but for the most part, the dogs of all different breeds were strangely, traumatically silent.

Muley, Stooge and Raven worked together to hitch up the team.

Muley turned them around in the big yard in front of what had been the shed.

"They are beautiful," Mary Rose said.

"Magnificent," Robbie added.

"Impressive," Hadley chimed in.

"Worthwhile," Marge said.

"And not half bad even if they are half-assed," Wiley grinned.

Alphonso and Raven nodded.

The mules clomped out of the driveway, headed for the animal shelter that was waiting for the rescued dogs.

The friends climbed into Alphonso's van and he started the engine.

"Wait!" Robbie said. "Where's Clyde?"

They looked around. In just a minute, Clyde appeared, running away from the shed as fast as his short little legs would carry him.

"He looks like the Energizer Bunny," Robbie said. Behind him, they heard a short blast and could see the shed burst into a bright blaze.

"He's burning down the shed!" Hadley said.

"That's arson!" Mary Rose added.

"I didn't see a thing," Marge said, looking the other way as Raven reached out the open door to grab Clyde and help him scramble into the van.

"Will this get you in trouble, Marge?" Hadley asked as they turned out of the driveway toward Meadow Lakes.

"Nope," the retired homicide detective said with a knowing grin.

Wiley and Mary Rose

Wiley's clothes were soaking wet
That happened on the day they met
Cowboy boots, Stetson hat, brown leather vest
That's all that he wore when he looked his best.

Laundry room's a romantic place
To have a first meeting face-to-face.

Their love was early, strong and brave
They fought over chickens and robbed a grave
They went to the Sand Hills where Wiley cried
And Mary Rose saw where the Cheyenne had died
They met Willie Winkie, a Vampire and Witches
And Wiley fought any who called his girls Bitches
On a trip to Alaska Wiley bought a jade ring
A beautiful, tender and real gorgeous thing
He proposed without a dinner or cup
And not his knees – he couldn't get up
Love when you're old is like it was years ago
Warm and exciting with a soft, gentle glow.

Love fluttered in our hearts.

The honor of your presence is requested at our wedding

MARY ROSE & WILEY

The Arboretum

6:00 pm

"Where is he now?" Mary Rose asked.

"Behind those trees," Marge said.

"Dumb bastard," Wiley growled.

"Ummmph," Raven said.

"But what's he doing?" Robbie asked.

"When have we ever figured out what he's doing?" Hadley replied.

"How the hell did he get the keys to my mower?" Alphonso snarled. "I don't allow guns either and I bet that's not loaded."

They were standing with a group of other residents, watching Zed Zonker draw, write, create or wrestle something into the long December grass in the massive back lawn of Meadow Lakes Retirement Community.

He was on the huge John Deere riding mower that lived in a huge, attractive shed behind the apartment complex.

"I never looked at that beast up close," Wiley said over the roar of the mower's engine.

"He's gunning it too much," Alphonso answered, "and that's my $25,00 John Deere X758!"

"$25,000!" Wiley yelled. "That's more than a Volkswagen Golf! That's more than a used Mercedes!"

"It's the Mercedes of lawn mowers," Alphonso said, moving closer to Wiley. The sound of the mower's engine was getting louder. "That sucker has three-cylinder, liquid-cooled, 992 V-twin diesel engines with twenty-four horses. It has a digital dashboard, which is probably giving Zonker a headache. It has a snowplow attachment, a fertilizer spreader and great power-steering."

"It also has cup holders," Raven added.

The girls did eye rolls.

Three maintenance men stood, hands on hips, near where Zed Zonker was creating whatever it was that was going into the grass. They rushed out as soon as one of them heard the motor roar, and they stopped short when they saw that riding shotgun with Zed Zonker was - - a shotgun.

He lifted the gun, pointed it at them, and they stopped dead in their tracks. Now they just watched with interest.

Marge hurried inside, grabbed a pair of binoculars from Alphonso's lower desk drawer, and rushed back outside. She held them to her eyes and focused in on what Zed was trying to do.

"He's got what looks like a big 'W' inside what I think is a circle."

She looked harder.

Hadley squinted.

Robbie put a hand on her forehead to shade her eyes.

Mary Rose was standing on tip toes with one hand on Wiley's shoulder.

"Either that or a giant squiggle in a circle," Marge guessed. "The thing in the middle is terrible, but the circle is pretty good."

"That's because my X758 has the best turning ratio money can buy," Alphonso bragged.

"Here he comes!" Mary Rose yelled.

Like an aging bat out of hell, Zed Zonker floored the big mower and drew an almost straight line through the circle and what appeared to be a 'W' inside.

Hadley took the binoculars from Marge and looked through them.

"I think I know what it is," she said loudly enough for them to hear. "It's a big 'W' in a circle with a line through it. It's how you say 'No' – like the cigarette in a circle with a line from top corner to opposite bottom corner. Says 'No Smoking.'"

"He's saying, 'No W?'" Robbie said.

They were quiet for a few seconds.

"No 'W' – No Wedding!" Robbie exclaimed. "Zed Zonker doesn't want the wedding to take place."

They looked at each other.

Wiley and Mary Rose raised their eyebrows together.

"You know the best one of those 'No' signs I've seen," Robbie volunteered. "It was at Christmas one year when a house had a lighted 'L' in a circle with the diagonal line through it. It was hanging on the front door. It took me a minute, then I realized they were saying No-L or Noel."

She grinned at Hadley. "I may look online and see if I can get one for Christmas this year."

Raven shook his head.

They looked as Zed Zonker, a wicked, pleased smile on his face, zoomed across the "W" one more time, crossing it out twice, then turned the behemoth of a mower toward the shed.

The maintenance crew ran after him.

"Hate to admit it," Alphonso said, turning his canes toward the dining room door, where other residents were trapesing into the building. "Zonker's not a bad driver."

They followed the other residents in through the door leading to the dining room. In the background they could hear Zed Zonker gifting the maintenance crew with long, loud and selective curses.

Wedding plans went as all wedding plans do – up and down, in and out, on and off and the least of the worst. Things were pretty well decided, and Mary Rose and Wiley were pretty well looking forward to a delightful Winter Solstice Ceremony.

The strange thing happened just after lunch.

Everyone was gathered around table 12. The table of friends had been changed from one seating four to one seating seven or eight. While there were seven in the group, the eighth chair was often occupied by someone who needed company or who wanted to be part of a real community. After all, there's always from for one more at table 12.

"Excuse me," Mary Rose said as Jill, their server came around with the coffee pot to complement the pecan pie dessert. "I have to go to the bathroom."

"She announces," Robbie smiled, her eyes following her friend out the dining room doors and watching her head toward the ladies' room nearby in the hallway.

Mary Rose opened the big swinging door into the bathroom. The door opened easily and smoothly, since Alphonso made sure every door at Meadow Lakes could be opened with no problem by a resident or visitor in a wheelchair or on crutches.

He remembered a time when one of his teammates on the Kansas City Chiefs had ended up temporarily in a wheelchair from a serious back injury. The team wanted him on the sidelines to encourage and energize the team, so he was happily along on a road trip for a game away from home. The team staff had booked a hotel that advertised every room as "handicapped accessible." Everything was. Except for the door. They couldn't get the wheelchair through the hotel room door.

It had taught Alphonso a good lesson.

Meadow lakes apartments were all handicapped accessible and they all had wide doors.

As soon as the door closed behind Mary Rose McGill, she stopped short, gasped and put her hand over her mouth. She blinked twice, not believing what she saw.

On his knees, dressed in his best suit, holding a small ring with a large diamond in it, was Zed

Zonker. His wispy hair had been smoothed over his balding pate and he was shaking just a little.

"Mary Rose McGill, I've been waiting all through lunch for you to come in here," he complained. "I want you to marry me. I have twice as much money as Vondra and I'm twice the man."

Zed Zonker had the ring held out to Mary Rose in one hand and the other hand behind his back.

"Zed Zonker, you are proposing to me and you have your fingers crossed behind your back. I can see them in the mirror behind you."

"Do not," Zed lied. "I'm serious. And I'm lucky. I came in here and had to go pee. So. while I was peeing, I took the ring out and when I pulled it out of the little box, I dropped the box and it went down the toilet." He laughed. "Good thing I didn't drop the ring!" he said.

"That will probably stop up the toilet," Mary Rose observed.

There was a pause.

"Excuse me," Mary Rose said, "but this is urgent."

She went into a stall, closed the door, pulled down her panties and peed.

"If you had urinals in here, I wouldn't have lost the damn box," Zed Zonker mumbled loud enough for Mary Rose to hear.

Mary Rose straightened her skirt, flushed and walked out. Without a word, she went to the sink, washed her hands and dried them.

Zed Zonker was still on his knees holding the ring.

"McGill, I'm waiting for a 'yes' here," he said.

"It's a 'no'," Mary Rose answered, and she headed for the door.

"Wait a minute," Zed Zonker said, loudly. "I can't get up from here!"

Mary Rose looked at him on his knees and smiled. "Someone will have to go pee soon. There will be a little old lady or two or three who dash in here after lunch."

The door swung closed happily behind her.

Yee Haw! A Western Wedding

The Winter Solstice slipped in on bright sunshine and a few gentle snowflakes.

Hadley, Mary Rose and Marge stood, looking out at the bright expanse of lawn that surrounded Meadow Lakes Retirement Community.

It was *The Wedding Day.*

They were all dressed alike. Mary Rose's daughters helped with the planning (with only three major arguments, four minor disruptions, and just three hours of not speaking to each other). They told their mother they wanted to stand up with both Wiley and Mary Rose, not just be maids of honor. They planned to form a line with two on each side of the minister, facing the bride and groom.

The BOOB Girls would be the Matrons of Honor.

The Matrons of Honor were dressed just like Mary Rose, with the exception of their blouses. Even Marge, as large as she was, looked good in the outfit.

A Western Wedding was the chosen theme. The wedding would take place in the spacious dining room of Meadow Lakes, called The Arboretum.

Mary Rose would wear a red-checkered blouse, jeans skirt, red cowboy boots and a white Stetson hat. Wiley would dress exactly as he always did, but his jeans would be new, his white Stetson would be new, his shirt would match Mary Rose's and his legendary brown leather vest would be his signature attire.

The BOOB Girls would have blue-checked Western blouses to contrast with Mary Rose's red check. All the rest, right down to the red cowboy boots would be identical. Jeans skirts, white Stetsons and daisy bouquets.

Alphonso, who would stand up with Wiley, was dressed like the others. New jeans, red cowboy boots, matching shirt and vest. He didn't look natural in a white Stetson, but who cared? He stuck a small Kansas City Chiefs logo on the underside of the brim.

Wiley told Robbie, in private, that Raven would be standing up with him, too, but dressed in Apache ceremonial clothing, not the cowboy style.

Robbie thought it would be like a B-rated cowboys and Indians movie. The thought made her smile tenderly.

Then Raven disappeared. He told Robbie he had been called back to his ranch, but said it was no big deal. He promised to be back for the wedding. He left almost immediately after Wiley told her he would be part of the wedding party. She didn't like it, but what could she do?

Weddings!

Anyway, Dr. Robinson Leary was busy. She was spending hours on her computer. No one asked her what she was doing. Robinson Leary, PhD, was always researching something.

Mary Rose, her daughters and her attendants would all hold small, sweet bouquets of daisies, Mary Rose's favorite flower. Good choice too, because it was a favorite of all of theirs. Daisies also decorated the tables that held the cake and champagne. A large bouquet of the bright flowers was on an altar at the front of the big dining room. The alter was one of the long tables from the storeroom, draped in a long denim tablecloth with red bandanas folded over the front.

It looked great. All they needed was Trigger or Champion to stand beside it.

Wiley thought all it needed was an old Colt 45 laying by the daisy centerpiece and a glass with a Yard of Beer for communion.

Wouldn't happen.

Clyde had done his Leprechaun magic and used his techie equipment to create a beautiful, translucent rainbow that ran from one pot of gold filled with daisies to another on the opposite side of the altar.

"Do you know who the minister is?" Marge asked Hadley and Robbie.

"No," they said together.

"They just wouldn't tell us," Hadley said. "Wiley mentioned someone in one of their families."

"They wouldn't tell us and I'm afraid Raven won't be here. I KNOW he won't be here, or he would be here NOW. It's just a couple of hours away. He was called back to his ranch, on some emergency and he left so suddenly, I barely had time to say goodbye."

"We know," Marge sympathized. Raven had probably kissed her on the top of her head while she was typing full speed, said goodbye, and she had replied with, "ummmmph."

Robbie looked miserable and sad at the thought. "I've called and called and it just goes to voicemail," she said in a soft voice.

Grandma LaVeau wasn't answering, either.

Where are they when you need them?

Hadley and Marge nodded.

It wouldn't be the same with one of them missing. Come on, Grandma LaVaeu, a little insight here, please.

Robbie had taken a moment in her apartment before joining everyone in the dining room. She had tried to sense something from the voodoo queen, but nothing had come. Now she was trying again.

"Why is it," she wondered, "that those feelings come when you don't particularly want them, and when you want then, they won't come?"

Outside the window, huge snowflakes began to fall, the sun still shining brightly.

Alphonso had set up a speaker system and even now, two hours before the ceremony, soft wedding music and tunes and love songs were coming from a soft, tasteful orchestra.

"I bet this is one time Mary Rose won't allow Wiley to play, 'Up Against the Wall, Red-neck Mother'," Hadley grinned.

"Or 'Mothers Don't Let Your Babies Grow Up to be Cowboys,'" Robbie sang.

"Or Wiley's other favorite, 'Good Night, Ireee-nne,'" Hadley sang.

"Irene, goodnight Irene, I'll see you in my dreams," Robbie sang on, appropriately off key. They put their arms around each other and belted out the chorus.

Through the air came the soft, big-band sound of Glen Miller's, "Moonlight Serenade," followed by Hadley's favorite, "String of Pearls."

Alphonso had his tech department put together some of the great love songs of all time, and they sat a perfect stage for a perfect wedding.

Just as the familiar strains of, "When You Wish Upon a Star," began, the first guests arrived.

All the residents had been invited and they began to drift in the side doors of the dining room.

Chairs had been sat in long rows and on the side of each row, a stanchion reached four feet into the air to hold a bouquet of daisies. The soft scent of the spring flowers was a beautiful contrast to the gentle snow outside.

Hadley and Robbie went to the window to watch for the first guest. Who they saw walking up the sidewalk from the parking lot made them both gasp.

Hadley put her hand to her mouth and Robbie put her's over her heart.

Walking up the sidewalk, wearing tight jeans, a flannel shirt, a jeans jacket and minimum maintenance hair, was Maggie Patten.

"This is not possible," Robbie said.

"I may faint," Hadley whispered as Maggie Patten opened the door, strode in and looked around.

They rushed to her.

She smiled.

"Hello. I'm looking for," and she pulled out her smart phone and tapped 'notes.' "Hadley Joy Morris Whitfield, Robinson Leary or Mary Rose McGill."

Robbie and Hadley were speechless, then Robbie gave her head a quick shake and said, "This is Hadley and I'm Robbie - - uh, Robinson."

"Maggie Patten?" Hadley croaked.

"My mother," the young Maggie said. "I've been doing a lot on Ancestry.com, and after a whole lot of googleing I traced her to this place. Took me over a year to do it."

She grinned Maggie Patten's crooked grin.

Robbie was first to collect her wits.

"You're Maggie's daughter?"

"Right. She was a teenager when I was born, and she gave me up for adoption. She named me Margaret, and my parents kept that name." She paused. "Except I'm known as Megs."

Robbie and Hadley were on her like mother hens over a new chick. They huggee her so tight she took a deep breath and pulled away.

"I take it you're glad to see me?"

"Oh, yes!" They said together.

Megs looked at them and then at the room.

"You have something going on," she smiled. "I'll be here a few days. Shall I come back tomorrow?"

Hadley thought of how Mary Rose would react if she spotted who she thought was Maggie Patten in the audience.

"That would be good," she said. "Come for a long lunch."

"You have a brother?" Robbie said, a question in her voice.

A half-brother. Different fathers. I tracked him down, too. He's a medical missionary in South Africa."

"We have so much to tell you about your mother," Hadley said, taking Meg's hand.

"I want to know it all," the young Maggie said.

She smiled, gave them each a quick, careful hug and turned toward the door.

"Where will I find you when I come back tomorrow?" she asked.

"We're at table 12," Hadley and Robbie said together.

Megs left and Robbie looked at her friend. Tears were running down Hadley's cheeks.

"Don't cry," Robbie said. "You'll have to re-do your makeup."

Hadley smiled and took her hand.

They turned toward the window and watched the Young Maggie walk back to her jeep.

The sun had come from behind a cloud.

They continued to watch.

"Look!" Robbie exclaimed. "Look!" And she pointed out the window toward the big circle drive that led to the front door.

A black Lincoln Town Car pulled to a stop in front of the big, double doors of the complex.

"Looks like FBI," Marge said as she moved up beside them.

"Try CIA," Hadley said, as two figures emerged from the back seat. One was a small, wiry woman with short white hair and a long black dress with a white lace collar. She was carrying a large, black, cumbersome handbag. A huge watch wrapped around her right wrist.

"Looks like a Ruth Bader Ginsburg wannabe," Marge smiled.

Stepping out of the other side of the sedan was a thin man dressed in white. His pants were white, his shoes were white, and his white tuxedo jacket covered a starched-stiff white shirt topped with a white bowtie.

On his head was a perfectly shaped aluminum foil hat with a sharp point on the top.

"Calamity Doodles and Leonard!" Hadley and Robbie exclaimed together.

Calamity Doodles. AKA Patty Whack, had come to Meadow Lakes in 2010 as a retired, undercover CIA agent whose mission was to find a hidden microchip in a gangster's mansion in west Omaha. The BOOB Boys, The Burned Old Bastards, had been residents at Meadow Lakes with their Aunt, Evangeline Goldberg. Calamity, who had introduced herself as Patty Whack when she first moved in, had found the microchip, friendship and Leonard.

She and Leonard were the ones who ran off and joined the circus. Calamity's father had been a circus clown and her mother the star of the circus wild west show. Thus, her real name, Calamity Doodles.

Calamity and Leonard walked up the wide sidewalk to the front entrance, Calamity's hand on Leonard's arm like a pair of royalty.

Just as they made it through the main door to the dining room, Clyde appeared, saw his brother and made a mad dash across the room, knocking over one chair and upsetting one of the daisy bouquets stanchions.

He took a running jump into his brother's arms and both of them went down onto the carpeted floor with a loud, 'thud'.

Calamity reached down. With the strength of a weightlifter, she pulled Clyde off Leonard, stood him upright, and gave him a smothering hug.

Leonard reached over, pulled a chair close to himself, and used it as a brace to lift himself upright.

"Clyde!"

"Leonard!"

"Calamity!"

Hugfest!

Clyde led Calamity and Leonard over to Marge and introduced them.

Marge, Omaha Police Department retired, towered over Calamity Doodles, CIA retired, but that didn't matter. The two women sat down together and talked as if they were old friends. Leonard and Clyde began to catch up while sitting at one of the tables. Hadley was relieved they hadn't decided to stay seated on the floor.

She had seen that happen before.

They talked of their brothers who had died, Robert and Rueben, the other two BOOB Boys, and of their beloved Aunt Evangeline, who made the best cinnamon rolls in the world.

Aunt Evangeline had died, too,but she had passed her secret recipe on to Clyde, who had been at work for three days creating a thirteen-layer cinnamon roll cake, which was going to be a beautiful centerpiece for the main refreshment table.

The cake, of course, would be surrounded by daisies.

Hadley looked at Robbie. "That's what you were doing at your computer when we had to keep calling you to come to lunch or dinner. She put her arm around her friend. "You were tracking down all the people we've loved these last twelve years."

"Hadley," a voice said behind her.

"Ed McGillicuddy, my favorite retinal specialist!"

Ed, also known as "McGill," exactly the same as Mary Rose, also treated Wiley for early macular degeneration. Wiley, unlike Hadley, had never fainted over a shot in the eye.

A shot in the eye!!

Ed and his wife, Beth, made their way through the crowd gathering in the dining room.

"Look!" Marge exclaimed again.

Pulling up in the circle drive was the most glamorous gypsy wagon imaginable. The horses, prancing and bobbing their heads up and down, were pure white. Their silver and gold harnesses were covered with sliver sleigh bells. White silk streamers flew from the top and sides of the wagon. The team was a perfect fit for the red, yellow and orange wagon, which had seats for eight inside a clear, transparent cover. Perfect for a celebratory ride around the grounds after the wedding.

A valet took the reins and a second helped a beautiful, white-haired gypsy down from the driver's seat. She was dressed to match the wagon, in red, yellow and orange, with silver boots and a bright red cape.

"Esmeralda St Benedict!" the girls yelled as she floated into the dining room.

There were more hugs.

"How in the world did you find her?" Hadley asked Robbie.

"I had a little help from my grandmother," Robbie smiled.

And where was that help now, when she wanted to track down an Apache? She went into a corner and called his cell phone again.

No answer.

"Okay," Marge said, looking through the windows again. "Who the hell wears a black hoodie to a wedding and who else wears a black suit that makes him look like an undertaker?"

They rushed to the window. There was an undertaker, a hooded companion and an attractive young woman with her arm through the undertaker's.

"Oh," Hadley said, looking at Marge, "remember Morgan Graves, who is an undertaker at Billow DeGround Funeral Home and Crematorium?"

"And the one in the hoodie would have to be Sam the Vampire," Robbie said.

The hoodie was of a very expensive and dressy light-weight leather.

"I didn't think we knew Morgan enough to invite him," Marge mused.

"He kind of takes care of Sam when he goes out in the daytime," Robbie explained. "Sam tends to twinkle when the sun hits him. And the lady, of course, is Mausie Lium, the bartender at Viva La Crypt Tavern."

Morgan walked into the room slowly, but Sam made a beeline for Hadley and hugged her hard.

"Sam!" She giggled.

"Are you still working at Happy Hollow Country Club at night and living with Morgan during the day?" Robbie asked, getting her hug.

Marge came over for a handshake.

She had never been into vampires.

"I am," Sam grinned, not letting go of Marge's hand, "and I moved into an oversized casket at Morgan's, so I'm much more comfortable. And I'm totally vegetarian now. No humans at all. Just wild animals." He winked at Marge as he let her go.

They were pleased.

Not all vampires do so well.

Willie Winkie arrived wearing a self-designed blue silk tuxedo with navy wingtip shoes, a navy bowtie and navy top hat. He was only inches taller than Clyde the Midget.

"He looks like a miniature pimp," Marge laughed. Willie shook hands.

He didn't hug.

It was just as well.

His nemesis, Dr. Fell was still in prison after attempting to kill Willie to take over his Winkie business of creating horrific Nightwear for Seasoned Women.

> I do not like thee, doctor Fell
> The reason why, I cannot tell
> But this I know and know full well.
> I do not like thee, doctor Fell.

The girls had been part of a fashion show in the Meadow Lakes dining room to showcase Willie's creations, which were basically the old baby doll pajamas, revisited.

The dining room had caught on fire.

It had been a good thing.

The remodeling was fantastic.

Guests milled around, and being a super host, Alphonso already had the champagne flowing, even before the wedding.

The guests milled, talked and laughed.

The girls watched the door.

They were first to see Ken David David and Denise pull up and get out of their red sports car.

It had been four years since Marge had tasered Ken David David when he had pretended to rob the bank at Salem's Crossing, Nebraska. They had ended up being his surrogate mothers and he had happily ended up being Denise's husband and a techie expert. He had gotten his degree, had gotten Denise and had also gotten a career as a Network Engineer for a large company in Lincoln, Nebraska.

The girls loved them both. At one time, they thought of giving Geoffrey to them, but didn't have the heart to let go of the big dog.

Denise carried a beautifully wrapped box for each of the BOOB Girls. It contained her delicious lemon bars which were wrapped in love.

The delicate green wrapping on each box matched Denise's lovely, long, hunter green, scoop-neck dress. She wore small diamond earrings that dangled just a short way from her ears and matched a delicate diamond necklace. Her matching green shoes made her the perfectly-attired wedding guest.

Ken David David looked like a normal, handsome guy in a suit.

"There she is!" Hadley cried. "Robbie, you did a terrific job with the guest list!"

A bright orange snowmobile pulled up to the front door. A valet reached out to offer a hand to the tall, slim lady dressed in a deep purple Vera Wang pantsuit and matching coat.

Chaos Cauldron walked majestically through the front door and into the dining room.

Chaos had lived at Meadow Lakes three years ago while she was a voodoo queen in training. Not with her, to Hadley's relief, were her three familiars: the white rats, Double Double, Toil and Trouble.

Chaos knew that voodoo queens didn't have familiars. That of course, was for witches. She didn't care and had crocheted tiny sweaters for her big, fat rats.

Geoffrey's opinion of nose-twitching, fuzzy, white competitors was simply, "Rats!"

"We've got to introduce her to Esmeralda!" Hadley said, and Robbie hurried toward where Esmeralda stood, talking to Alphonso.

She overheard their conversation as she approached. Esmeralda was smiling. "I do like football, Alphonso. Eet ees such a lively contact sport."

"My dear," Alphonso said, "football is NOT a contact sport. Football is a collision sport. Dancing is a contact sport."

"I'm pulling her away," Robbie told Alphonso, and she led Esmeralda over to Chaos Cauldon, who was getting more than one hug from Hadley and Marge.

"Chaos Cauldron, this is Esmeralda St Benedict. Boy, do you two have a lot in common."

As if they had known each other for years, the two magical women, embraced.

"They are. indeed, magical women," Robbie observed.

"Every woman has magical friends," Hadley said. "Most of the time we don't recognize them or our own magic."

Chaos, who was in reality, Doctor Cauldron, had directed them in looking at their backstories and who they really were.

And who they were ow were beautiful, mature women who had stretched their prime out for years in a joyous, graceful manner.

"Grace. Humor. Courage and Confidence," Hadley would often say.

In their growing up, the BOOB Girls had been an abuscd daughtcr of an alcoholic fathcr, a replacement child of a child who died, a homeless teenager and the great-granddaughter of the world's most beautiful voodoo queen of New Orleans.

They had shared all this because of Chaos, who was now deep in conversation with Esmeralda.

Robbie looked at her phone to check the time.

Five minutes until the ceremony.

Raven was not going to make it.

She sighed, shook her head and slipped the phone back into her pocket.

Last to arrive were Mark, Molly and Rachael from Marks Bistro, where the gun, found in a galvanized bucket filled with concrete and buried beneath a crabapple tree at Marks Bistro, led them on an adventure back in time to the Omaha of 1898.

The friends had gathered.

The rows of chairs that filled the dining room were full.

The soft music of Glen Miller floated through the air.

It was interrupted.

There was a pause.

Harry James' big band began to roll out "Sentimental Journey" on the system.

The girls hurried to the front of the dining room and stood in their positions by the altar.

Mary Rose's daughters walked through the side door and took their place in their carefully rehearsed line behind the altar. Like the girls, they were dressed in western wear complete with the red boots.

Robbie watched the door, then gasped and put her and to her heart, nearly dropping her bouquet of daisies.

Raven led Wiley and Alphonso through the door and into the ceremonial area. He was dressed in white buckskin with white moccasins. There was a white silk headband around his head as all Apaches wore, and it held five white feathers to symbolize his name; Raven Five Horns and designate him as a descendant of a chief.

Of course, Robbie thought, *as a hereditary chief, he can perform ceremonies.*

She swelled with pride and looked harder at the oversized collar that connected the white buckskin shirt from his chest to his neck. It was covered with a beautiful array of gems and beads. It was intricately woven. Around his neck hung a large turquoise medallion wrapped in shining silver. The emblem of a chief? It was precious. In his hands, Raven carried a white-bound book.

The wedding party turned toward the back of the room, and through the open doors came the bride. The guests rose and turned, smiles covering their faces.

Mary Rose McGill in her red-checked shirt, red boots, denim skirt and white Stetson began to walk to the altar. What the girls could see around the white Stetson, showed her hair to be perfect, her make-up was perfect, and she had a perfect escort down the aisle.

Geoffrey, newly bathed and without a leash, was walking alongside his lady with only a tiny limp. Around his neck he wore a new red collar and a larger collar of daisies. He was so clean his fur gleamed, and he looked proud.

Certainly, as proud as a dog can look.

Hands reached out to Mary Rose as she walked slowly down the aisle. She smiled a beautiful, wide smile as she touched the hands of Esmeralda St Benedict, Chaos Cauldron, Calamity Doodles and Denise.

"I've never seen a bride do that before," Marge whispered to Hadley.

"You've never seen a bride escorted by a mastiff wearing daisies before, either," Hadley smiled.

Mary Rose walked slowly up to the altar, then turned and faced her bridegroom.

Wiley was beaming. He removed his hat and handed it to Alphonso.

Geoffrey did his Olympic class sit beside the bride. He looked like a large statue of a big dog with a daisy wreath around his neck. He didn't move during the entire ceremony.

Harry James' "Sentimental Journey" turned into a barely audible series of beautiful soft notes, played Hadley thought, on and Indian flute. It was perfect, too.

Raven began as always at weddings: *Dearly Beloved, we are here....*

At the same time, Robbie, Marge and Hadley felt a single tear roll down their cheeks.

When it came time for vows to be exchanged, the room was totally silent except for the gentle notes of the flute.

Raven looked at Wiley.

Mary Rose, this is a first for me. It was a first when I first saw you and it was a first when I first fell in love with you.

"Definitely a first," Hadley whispered.

This is the last chapter of our lives and I am honored and proud and the luckiest man in the world to be your husband. I love you, Mary Rose McGill, and I will take care of you and honor you and be yours for as long as I live.

Wiley slipped the ring onto her finger.

Wiley, It's a first for me, too. I learned from you what it was to be brave, to take risks and to not let life go by without grabbing it by the tail. When I had cancer, it was you who held me and helped me cry and I knew you would be there for as long as we live. I love you, Wiley Vondra and I will be your helpmate and take care of you all the days of my life.

Mary Rose slipped a plain silver band onto Wiley's finger.

Raven led the couple in all the usual "I do's."

Now, Raven said, *it is my honor to give you a little bit of my culture to start you on your new Sentimental Journey.*

He looked lovingly at Wiley and Mary Rose. He knew the prayer by heart.

Now you will feel no rain,
For each of you will be shelter for the other.
Now you will feel no cold,
For each of you will be warmth to the other.
Now there will be no loneliness,
For each of you will be companion to the other.
Now you are two persons,
But there are three lives before you: his life,
her life and your life together.
Go now to your dwelling place
to enter into your days together.
And may all your days be good and long upon the Earth.

Mary Rose's four Marys broke into an unusually good version of *Sentimental Journey* as Raven took hold of the hands of the bride and groom and turned them around to face their room full of witnesses, a room full of people who loved them. "I present to you, Mr. and Mrs. Wiley and Mary Rose McGill Vondra."

The crowd rose and the room filled with applause and cheers.

The newlyweds raised their arms in a salute and arm in arm, as the crowd continued to applaud and cheer, they slowly walked down the aisle. Mary Rose's daughters sang them all the way to the back of the room.

Geoffrey, looking as if he were proud of the four rows of daisies around his neck, followed them. He could smell the cinnamon roll cake that was being carried out to the serving table.

"There goes her pension," Zed Zonker said to the man standing next to him.

Sentimental Journey

Robbie hugged Raven so hard his ribs hurt.

"I was afraid you wouldn't come!"

"Wouldn't miss it for the world."

"They wouldn't tell me you for officiating!"

Raven grinned and patted her back. He was still holding her, and she was still liking it.

She smiled a gorgeous smile. "I love the Apache Blessing."

"Guess what," Raven smiled back. "It's not Apache. We stole it from a book by a Elliott Arnold. *Blood Brother*."

"Who cares?"

"Take all the credit you can get," Raven replied, kissing the top of her head.

The serving table was topped with layers of cinnamon rolls, making a cinnamon roll cake. A couple with a dog graced the top as a fun wedding ornament.

The tablecloth, like the one on the altar, was denim and cowboy bandanas decorated the edges and served as keepsake napkins.

The music was back at Glen Miller. It was drowned out by the laughter and happy chatter.

Toasts were touching and sweet and brought tears to the crowd's eyes.

"Remember that toast Mary Rose gave when Chaos lived here?" Robbie asked Hadley.

Hadley smiled and motioned for Raven to move in closer to hear.

"Mary Rose said, and she really did say this, 'I don't drink much, two at the most. Three I'm under the table and four I'm under the host.'"

"Tell her to give that one now, since Wiley's the host," Robbie laughed.

Raven smiled and shook his head.

Mary Rose and Wiley hugged all the unexpected surprise guests. They knew it was Robbie who had worked real magic getting them all together.

Robbie was pleased watching Mary Rose's excitement as she hugged each old friend.

The biggest surprise came when Mary Rose finally got time to fill her small plate with cinnamon rolls and goodies. A shadow appeared beside her, and sure it was Wiley, she said, "These boots are killing my feet."

There was no answer.

She finished gathering her refreshments and turned around. A man of medium height, white beard and beautiful long white hair stood smiling at her. He was older than she and instead of a cane, he had a walking stick...a genuine, wooden walking stick. His suit was western, fitting the occasion, and he had what looked like alligator boots.

He continued to smile, not saying anything.

Mary Rose looked at him.

She knew him, but who was he?

She looked at his mouth and the way his eyes were set under his brows. He made her think for just a second of her father.

Her father…

"Teddy!" she yelled. Her plate clattered to the floor, sending her cinnamon rolls and tiny mints flying.

"Hi Sis," the man smiled. "Congratulations to ye."

One of the servers hurried over to pick up Mary Rose's plate.

Wiley hurried to her side.

The entire assembly turned to watch.

"Wiley! This is my brother! I haven't seen him since I was fifteen and he saved me when our father tried to rape me."

She was holding onto the man as if he might disappear again.

The crowd smiled, then went back to friendly conversation and laughter.

"The last thing I saw that day was Teddy here, going out the door with his packed-full duffle bag." She slipped her arm around her brother's waist. "I remember how your sneakers were tied on and hanging over the side," she said, looking at him with tears in her eyes.

Wiley gave him a hug and he hugged back.

"I was in California," Teddy said, "then a few months ago this crusty old geezer," he thought for a second. "Zed something."

"Zonker," Wiley and Mary Rose said together.

"Aye. He came to a resort where I was stayin' as part of a golf tournament. We sat on the veranda, had a drink, and he started talking about Omaha and this lady named Mary Rose. I listened. I put two and two together and decided it was time to get back together. I did some research, leaned it was you and found out about the wedding."

Mary Rose noticed the slight, most attractive accent when her brother spoke.

They were grinning from ear to ear. The friends were all gathering to meet Mary Rose's brother who had disappeared after rescuing her when they were teenagers.

They all met Teddy, then Marge hurried across the room to hug a late comer. Buckshot Betsy Bushwhacker had slipped in unnoticed. She wore what she usually wore when she dressed up in her hometown of Gospel Bird, Alaska, which was a long western dress, black boots and an Indian necklace on top of a red bandana tied around her neck.

They rescued Buckshot Betsy after she wrote to her cousin, Marge Aaron, telling her that she had been arrested for the murder of her longtime lover, Pickaxe Pete. Even by the time they buried him, no one in Gospel Bird remembered his real name.

She shot him through the door, which Hadley claimed was much better than shooting him through the balls. Betsy's defense had been that he was wearing lifts in his shoes, which made him taller. She had aimed above his head.

She was obviously not a lawyer.

They had gotten her acquitted and the judge went fishing with Raven and the boys.

Good-bye

Out-of-town guests were staying at a nice motel near Meadow Lakes. Tomorrow would be a day of reminiscing and laughter as everyone caught up. After that, Wiley and Mary Rose would begin a new Sentimental Journey together.

Now, however, Alphonso was helping Marge into the beautiful gypsy wagon that had the magnificent horses and an equally magnificent Esmeralda St Benedict at the reins. The horses were prancing in place and their sleigh bells could be heard all over the grounds.

The snow was falling slowly, in big flakes.

"Looks like a Norman Rockwell Christmas," Hadley said as she climbed in.

Hadley, Robbie and Raven snuggled under bright red blankets in the back seat. Ahead of them sat Alphonso and Marge, Marge's red cane draped casually over an unusually convenient hook on the side of the carriage. Their blankets were bright yellow. Wiley and Mary Rose sat directly behind Esmeralda and were snuggled under bright white blankets.

Mary Rose still held her bouquet of daisies and she held Wiley's hand as well.

Geoffrey, who still had his daisies around his neck, sat straight and proud next to Mary Rose. A valet had lovingly lifted his rear to help him into the carriage.

Zed Zonker watched from his third-floor apartment window. He was holding a glass of champagne in one hand and the expensive bottle in the other. He had stolen the bottle in great stealth and cleverness as he slid out of the reception.

Three of Meadow Lakes servers had watched him and shaken their heads. The cost would appear on his rent receipt the following month.

"Gonna be a friggin blizzard tonight," he said to himself.

He raised his glass to the friends in the colorful wagon with the joyful sleigh bells. He kept it raised while they disappeared around the corner of Meadow Lakes and out of sight.

Zed Zonker closed his curtains and sat down.

The gypsy wagon continued on, sleigh bells singing in the winter air.

They were out of sight now.

And they lived on with Grace, Humor, Courage and Confidence.

For the rest of their lives.

The End

REFLECTIONS FROM THE GIRLS

Micah 6
And what does the Lord require of you
But to do justice,
To love mercy,
And to walk humbly with your God.

The wisest thing I've told my grandchildren is: "When you feel anxious about something – change the word 'anxious' to 'excited' and your outlook becomes heathier and different."

Paris, my beautiful granddaughter, and I were having lunch and she said, "Nama, you know what the most important thing is you've ever told me?"

Here it comes - - change "anxious" to "excited." I was waiting to hear it.

"You said if I didn't like a book, I didn't have to finish it, and that's the most important thing you've ever said to me."

Okay.

So, if you want to stay with the BOOB Girls, comedy mystery novels for older women, and skip a few pages and go straight to "A Note From Joy," that may be the most important thing I'll say to you – just stay with the stories of these Burned Out Old Broads at Table 12.

Or you may read on. These are my reflections, spoken through the girls but spoken with my voice for justice and mercy. Some of you will agree and cheer, some of you will scoff, some of you will be surprised and some of you will slam the book shut ad think I had no business putting all that into print.

The choice is yours.

Then again – it may be exciting.

If you have a voice, use it

If it speaks for justice

If it speaks for mercy

If it speaks for the goodness of the world

Use your voice.

REFLECTIONS FROM ROBBIE

Southern Trees bear strange fruit

Blood on the leaves and blood at the roots,

Black body swinging in the Southern breeze,

Strange fruit hanging from the Poplar tree.

Pastoral scene of the gallant south.

The bulging eyes and the twisted mouth.

Scent of magnolias, sweet and fresh

Then the sudden smell of burning flesh.

Here is a fruit for the crows to pluck.

For the rain to gather,

for the wind to suck.

For the sun to rot,

for the trees to drop.

Here is a strange and bitter crop.

Bill Holiday's signature song,
written by Abel Meeropol

Robbie

"No Negro deserves an A."

Dr. Robinson Leary, PhD, Phi Beta Kappa,
couldn't spring upright in bed anymore when
the dream haunted her sleep. She used to wake
up sitting bolt upright, wet with sweat. Now her
body didn't cooperate like it had when she was
fifteen years younger. But the dream was the
same, a replay of a reality that had jarred Robbie
to her fingertips.

She had been in Mr. Larson's high school English
class and had perfect scores on everything she
had done from homework to class participation to
test after test. And now she was standing in front
of his desk, hands shaking and formed into fists,
asking him to explain the B on her report card.
In all four years of high school she had gotten
straight A's. Honor society. Principal's List. In
college it would have been a perfect 4-point
average.

But no Negro deserves an A.

It was prejudice, pure and simple. It was Jim
Crow of the grade point.

Some of the class heard about it and the word went through the school like hotdogs at lunch on Monday.

Robbie knew her father would come and talk to the principal, Mr. Drawyers. Chester Drawyers. That's when Robinson Leary began to groan at funny names. Her father would put on his suit, not wear his work clothes, and walk to the school.

Mr. Drawyers would change the grade.

Mr. Drawyers would not mention it or say anything to Mr. Larson.

Her friends didn't like it. Neither one of them. There were only two. She was the only Negro in the school in the small town where she grew up.

She had been the only student in the entire history of the school who had been allowed – no, make that forced – to go to the prom with someone not enrolled in the high school. She had to invite a Negro boy, so she had invited her mother's cousin's son from Omaha to be her date. He had obliged. She had a blue satin dress and she looked beautiful. He was handsome in his tux. She joked that she was the only girl at the dance who could actually say her date was, "tall, dark and handsome."

Today, decades later, she was Dr. Leary, retired full professor from Creighton University, scholar, mentor and best friends with three white women: The BOOB Girls.

The lesson taught by Mr. Larson's B, was how to take a stand for social justice. Her father had talked, and only once, about barely missing a lynching. In the South, where he was raised, Sunday lynchings of black men, women and children were entertainment for the white Christians coming from church. Her doctoral thesis had been, "The Impact of Lynching Spectacles on American Literature."

There hadn't been much to research, but she researched every bit she could find. White theologians pretty much ignored it. Black preachers didn't write a lot about it. There were few books and a few more speeches that had been printed, many of them by gutsy women who were threatened with lynching for speaking out.

It was no big deal to torture and lynch women and children.

Robbie had made an assignment for her English class at Creighton, and she thought of it now.

She slipped out of bed carefully and quietly. Raven was asleep on his back, breathing softly. She had been asleep with her head on his chest and now she gently covered him up, then turned, slipped out of bed, put on her soft pink robe and white satin slippers. Without making a sound, she walked to the big desk in her apartment's second bedroom, the room which she called her "study."

She dug around in the files carefully hung on file rods in the big bottom left drawer of her massive roll-top desk. She found the folder labeled, *Strange Fruit*.

On the outside of the folder, carefully drawn, was an outline of a tree in full leaf. The trunk was wide enough for song lyrics to fit neatly into it. It was Abel Meeropol's, (also known as Lewis Allen) song with which Billie Holiday – Lady Day – finished each concert. She would hold a white carnation and raise her fantastic voice in gentle, mournful, plaintive song:

Southern Trees bear strange fruit
Blood on the leaves and blood at the roots,

Black body swinging in the Southern breeze,
Strange fruit hanging from the Poplar tree.

Pastoral scene of the gallant south.
The bulging eyes and the twisted mouth.
Scent of magnolias, sweet and fresh
Then the sudden smell of burning flesh.
Here is a fruit for the crows to pluck.
For the rain to gather,
for the wind to suck.
For the sun to rot, ·
for the trees to drop.
Here is a strange and bitter crop.

Robbie sat in a comfortable chair in front of the window next to her desk, put the file on her lap and lovingly ran her hand over it. Outside, the wind had picked up and small drifts of new-fallen snow climbed the wall under her widow.

"Strange fruit hanging from the Poplar tree," she whispered.

Her eyes softly filled with tears. She debated whether to open the file on her lap. It was old now. The file cover had hardened with age, but what was inside was as new as the latest protest march, the newest sunrise. Inside was a lesson plan, a simple assignment she had used every year. She opened the folder and read:

Lynching: Named after Judge Charles Lynch who, during the Revolutionary War, sentenced British supporters to be hung from trees.

Reference: James H. Cone, professor of theology, Union Seminary, New York.

James H. Cone is thought to be the creator of Liberation Theology and this is one of his quotes: "But doing theology with little recognition or regard for the oppressed was and, for the most part still is, the practice of "theology" in America. I have often found it so revealing that the required "theology courses" in most seminaries, universities, and majority churches are indeed white and Western, while all the "liberation theologies" are thought to be extracurricular and optional electives. The real theology is still assumed to be Euro-American and male; changing that will be key to the transformation most needed to align America and Europe with the center of the church that has now moved decisively to the global South."

"So much for Mary Magdalene being recognized as the only chosen witness to the resurrection, the most beloved disciple and probably married to Jesus as well as being a wealthy Jewish lady and never a prostitute," Robbie thought when she first read Cone's statement.

This is one of the true stories Cone told his classes:

Valdosa, Georgia, 1918

Haynes Turner was lynched because it was known that he did not like his white boss. Haynes' wife, Mary, was eight months pregnant with a baby they had wanted and for whom they had prayed and for whom they had waited. They were young and in love.

Mary protested Haynes' lynching, was vocal about it and vowed to seek justice.

As a result, the sheriff arrested Mary, the mob stripped her naked, hung her upside down by her ankles, finding a strong branch fairly close to the ground. They soaked her in kerosene then set her on fire. She literally roasted to death.

A man in the mob, still wearing his church clothes from his white, Christian church, took out a hunting knife, slit open her pregnant belly, pulled the baby out and stomped it to death, being careful not to get anything on his good church pants.

Your assignment, as English literature students, is to express your feelings and thoughts about this incident by writing a two-page letter to one of the following:
Mary Turner
Haynes Turner
The man who stomped the baby to death
A woman in the crowd
A child in the crowd
The Sheriff
The pastor of the white church where most of the mob were members
And of course, Mary and Haynes' baby.

You may write more than, but not less than, two pages and your writing must reflect impact, sentiment and how this story related to YOU. Feel free to use Biblical text to prove your point. Robbie sat with her hands on the open file.

Beneath them were pages of aging, hand-written letters, most of them to Mary. Some of them – all by girls – were to the baby.

The girls in her Creighton University class were all shocked and saddened and nearly overwhelmed. The white boys in the class were enraged and every black student, male or female, was overwhelmed and some could not write a letter at all.

The exercise had been so powerful that Robbie started inviting a counselor – African American – to conduct the next day's class. That was a good idea.

Robbie knew now that James H. Cone died in 2018 and that his story had found its way, along with many others, into his award-winning book, *The Cross and the Lynching Tree*. The book would become a best-seller. It showed clearly that black men, women and children had been not just 'lynched.' They had been *crucified*.

The book told how the black victim's fingers, toes, genitals and ears had been cut off and sold to the mob.

It told how a photographer was present at the "Lynching Spectacle" and sold picture postcards. One postcard with a picture of a burned body hanging from a tree, had been sent to a relative with the words, "Guess what we had for barbeque last night."

The Cross and the Lynching Tree was here, in Robbie's study, and it lay now in a special place on her desk. The yellow leaves on the tree in the cover picture fit perfectly into the yellow and blue décor of her study. The book deserved to be displayed.

The storm outside had grown angry and the wind was blowing snow hard against Robbie's window. There was enough ice mixed with the snow to make an annoying, raspy, scratching sound.

Dr. Leary thought about the time, just a couple of months ago, when she had taken The BOOB Girls to a symposium at the courthouse in Omaha. It was a symposium to commemorate the one hundredth-year anniversary of the September 1919 hanging in Omaha of Will Brown, a young black man guilty of nothing.

A stage play, *Red Sumer*, had played at the Blue Barn theater and was a success. As was the symposium where busloads of high school students, wearing their school shirts, arrived and walked across the ground where Will Brown's burned body lay after he was lynched from a pole on the courthouse grounds.

The black undertaker had sworn his body was riddled by more than one thousand bullet holes.

The young people had listened to the speakers, many with their mouths open when it was announced by the head of Black Studies at Creighton University, that it was not until 2005 that the US Senate issued an apology for not passing anti-lynching laws. The reason for not passing such legislation was that according to southern legislators, "lynching was necessary to guarantee the purity of the white race in the south."

Thinking that made Robbie snicker.

She wondered, as she often had, if the grandson of the soulless man who tore Mary Turner's baby from its safe, warm womb, was the feelingless man whose picture was taken, smoking a cigar and leaning against a mailbox outside a woman's clinic. His foot rested on a small box designed as a baby's casket. His sign, leaning against the mailbox, read, "Baby Killers!"

Yep – they were probably related, especially as he waved that sign at women going in to get mammograms as well.

Robbie stood up, looked out at the vicious storm, turned and put the file back in the drawer. She would slip back onto Raven's shoulder and hope she could go to sleep.

Raven. He knew a lot about prejudice, too. His people had pretty much been eliminated by white genocide.

Robbie smiled as she padded softly through the study door towards her bedroom.

The wind outside moaned a long, sad moan as it wandered around the corner of the building. It was picking up some.

She had given every student doing this assignment an A.

Black and white, red, yellow and brown – all kids deserve A's.

REFLECTIONS FROM HADLEY

"Do ya need a little help?"

I turned and smiled at him.

He was tall, with white hair, white beard
and a well-used pipe sticking out of his pocket.

He had a soft Scottish accent.

I was walking slowly down the huge corridor
between planes,

Trying not to limp as I pulled my carry-on bag
awkwardly behind me.

Hip hurting. Back aching. Bag squeaking.

Head throbbing. Heart beating too fast.

I broke into a sweet, fake Scottish brogue.

"Only if ya can make me 10 years younger and 5
pounds lighter," I smiled.

He laughed.

He was from Scotland, but lived in Manhattan in a neighborhood that spelled money.

And he offered me his arm.

I took it.

We walked slowly.

We talked and laughed until we came to a crossroads.

We stopped and looked at each other.

We hugged for a long time.

He went right. I went left.

Hip hurting. Back aching. Bag squeaking.

Head throbbing. Heart beating too fast.

"Do ya need a little help?"

Hadley

The big schoolhouse Regulator clock on the wall by Hadley's bed held both hands straight on 1a.m.

Tick tock, tick tock.

Big pendulum swinging back and forth, back and forth, back and forth.

She threw her legs over the side of the bed and sat there for a minute. She looked at the clock again, then slowly stood up, grabbed her phone, slipped into her warm, fuzzy slippers and her soft robe with the big pockets. The phone dropped into one pocket. She looked at the clock one more time.

"As long as I'm awake, I might as well do something productive," she said to the clock. "I'll go pee."

The clock agreed and tocked again.

She smiled, then padded off to the bathroom.

Maintenance insomnia with phantom sleep.

She read about it.

She had it.

She was good at self-diagnosis.

She could go to sleep right away. She was, almost every night, following the old saying, "Asleep before her head hit the pillow."

And for the first two or three hours, she slept beautifully.

Then she woke up.

Sometimes she would be awake for more than an hour, sometimes longer, sometimes less.

The disconcerting thing was, sometimes she thought she had been awake all that time she had lain in bed after coming back, and when she checked the lighted numbers on her bedside clock, it told her differently.

Sleeping when you think you're awake. Phantom sleep.

Because she had such a relationship with the night, she had adopted Robbie's attitude that Mother Night was her friend.

Her own mother must have had the same insomnia because she talked about vacuuming the house at two in the morning.

At two in the morning, Hadley read in her tablet. Mindless mysteries. Nothing serious. Reading for pleasure was a privilege she planned on enjoying for the rest of her life.

And she didn't know how long that would be.

Her tablet, phone, reading glasses and an "I will keep this cold and not even let your ice melt," thermos all waited for her on the little table by her bed. The table was constructed from giant coffee cups and plates stacked on top of each other. Marge described it as "art on steroids."

Hadley loved it.

In the bathroom, she washed her hands and pumped some lotion on them. The lotion sat in a fine porcelain bottle with an antique motif.

She looked at her hands.

"Ada's hands," she thought.

She had been like a clone of her Aunt Ada. They looked exactly and eerily alike. Once she had seen a picture of Ada and asked her mother when she had taken this picture of her.

The first thing she noticed about her Ada hands were the veins. They stuck up like healthy worms under her skin. The times she had needed an IV, the nurses had used those veins instead of the ones in her elbows, which won wimpy awards they were so small, rolling and hard to find.

Then she studied the wrinkles and creping. Two black sunspots had popped up on the left hand.

Long figures with acrylic nails. Those looked pretty good. Getting fake nails had been one of the best gifts she'd given herself. Wiggs, her nail tech of twenty plus years had said it well, "If somebody asks if those are your nails, you say, 'Damn right. I paid good money for 'em.'"

She didn't bother hurrying back to Wiggs now if a nail broke. She didn't care so much. She found the broken nail if she could, grabbed a tiny tube of super glue and when she got to table 12, asked one of the girls to glue it on for her.

She wasn't taking care of her appearance as much as she used to. She turned to the big mirror over the sink and frowned at herself. Well, after her shower she would put on her makeup, make sure her hair was behaving and pick out one of her better pantsuits. If Mary Rose McGill could claim ageless beauty, so could she.

She decided to read sitting in her recliner in the living room.

Tick tock, tick tock.

Throughout her apartment, Hadley had small, stylish signs. "You can read your way through my rooms," she happily informed people. Funny sayings that made her smile hung on nearly every wall along with her Tom Mangelsen wildlife photographs.

She read, "Old age is coming at a really bad time." That one was true for sure.

"Marriage is like a deck of cards. When you start out all you need are two hearts and a diamond. By the time it's over, you wish you had a club and a spade." That was her favorite.

Running a close second was a little sign you saw when you stood after using the bathroom. "If you're waiting for a sign, this is it."

There was the one Wes Longbow had given her. "May you laugh so hard tears run down your leg." Wes. One of the loves of her life who had died a few years ago.

Wes.

Hadley's tablet was in one big pocket on her robe and her phone in the other. She was making it a habit to always have her phone with her. Her balance wasn't as good as it had been, and sometimes she felt weak. She even put her phone on the floor by her shower when she bathed. Having her phone always with her, she didn't have to have one of those awful button things people wore around their necks to push in case they fell or had an emergency.

They were a good thing – life savers.

She just didn't want one.

Hadley walked noiselessly into the kitchen. She stuck a coffee pod into her magic coffee machine and waited while the smell filled the kitchen. Coffee didn't keep her awake. The dumb insomnia did.

The coffee trickled into the Disney mug her granddaughter had given her, the one with 'Grandma' written on the handle. The cup felt good and warm in her hands.

Her feet took her and her coffee to the window. The snowstorm had turned into a slow shower of giant, fluffy flakes, gradually building up across the beautiful grounds of the retirement community. It looked like a carpet of sparking white feathers.

"Now the winter of our discontent, made summer by this glorious sun of York." It was Hadley's favorite line from Shakespeare.

"Richard III," Robbie had reminded her more than once.

"This is the winter of our lives, too," Hadley said to the snow. The snow answered by a gentle wind blowing some against the window where she stood.

She took a sip of her coffee. It was steaming and delicious.

Hadley Joy Morris Whitfield considered herself extremely lucky. She was, all in all, healthy for her age, active with pretty good energy. And even though she was tired by late afternoon, did very little in the evening, and went to bed, sometimes as early as 8 p.m., she led a full, active life. More active than a lot of women ten years younger.

She had no complaints.

Yet......

She agreed that, "Growing old sucks." She had ruined a perfectly good Christian witness with that statement. It was at church, during coffee hour between services, and she was sitting at a table across from Leslie and her husband, Gordon. He was in his motorized wheelchair, oxygen at his side. Leslie was in her body brace with her walker next to her chair. Sitting beside Hadley was a healthcare worker in her fifties. Hadley did not know the lady's name.

Leslie was talking about Gordon coming home from the hospital after being severely dehydrated and how much she had to struggle to take care of them both. She wasn't complaining, just reporting.

Hadley shook her head when Leslie finished and said the famous line, "Growing old sucks." Leslie nodded.

The healthcare worker reached over, placing her hand on Hadley's arm where it rested on the table. It was just above the hand she was using to gently hold the handle of her coffee cup.

"Oh, no." The healthcare lady smiled one of those patronizing smiles we all know – the kind of smile that makes you want to strangle the person wearing it. "You are witnessing the transition from a life of pain and suffering here into one of comfort and peace beyond."

Hadley looked at her.

"That is the dumbest thing I've heard all morning," she said.

The healthcare worker hadn't sat with them again.

Hadley settled into her recliner by the window, sipping her coffee and glancing out again at the gentle, feathery snowfall. Next to her recliner hung another favorite sign. It was a picture of a cartoon Death, complete with scythe, cloak and cowl, looking down at a brush standing on skinny legs and who was looking up at the black figure whose features were lost in the cowl.

The line underneath it read, "A Brush with Death."

She read the line, smiled, and her mind began to wander. Outside, the wind blew a small fit of snow against her window.

She would die soon and have her own brush with Death. She looked lovingly at the little picture with the two cartoon figures. The cowl covered Death's face. Only the skeletal hands showed in the picture.

"You might as well come sit with me," she said to the cartoon Death. "Being this old, I'm in the Decade of Death."

In her mind, the little Death jumped out of the picture and perched on the armrest of her chair. She couldn't see the miniature skeletal face in her imagination, but she could tell Death was sitting with its legs crossed, by the way the black robe draped over its bony knees. The brush with its skinny little legs and wee eyes just stayed in the picture and watched.

It didn't want to miss anything.

Death looked friendly and cute sitting on her armrest.

She smiled again. Not such a scary figure.

"It doesn't matter how healthy I am right now," she told her little companion. "As Redd Foxx said, 'Health nuts are going to feel stupid someday, lying in the hospitals dying of nothing. Me, I plan to be sick when I die.'"

Tiny Death nodded in approval.

Death was a good listener.

"So, how will I die?" She asked. Death shrugged. "If I have a long illness, I'll be able to say goodbye and take care of business. With a sudden death, I could avoid a lot of pain, suffering and helplessness."

She thought for a minute. "Not to mention probably a fair bout of dread and depression."

When she looked at Death, it had taken a comfortable position sitting on her knee. It held the scythe straight up beside it. Very attentive, this Tiny Death. Very interested. Hadley abandoned her cup of coffee.

"My family died of cancer or heart disease." She paused as Tiny Death continued to listen. "Well, doesn't about everyone die of either cancer or heart disease?"

Death seemed to already know all that.

"If I die of a sudden heart attack it could interrupt a perfectly good lunch at Marks or happen here, alone in my apartment and that wouldn't be pleasant, either."

"My friend, Maureen, the counselor, said if something bothers us, we should 'name our demons'. Well, Death, you bother me, and you bring demons with you."

Hadley imaged several tiny red demons with horns wearing little red capes and bright red boots. They gathered around Tiny Death.

They seemed to be dancing.

"How about these?" She asked the little congregation sitting on her knee acting like long-lost friends at a school reunion. She began to name the demons.

"**Fear.** How do you like that? I'm afraid of being afraid."

The little group looked at her intently, Tiny Death's head was hidden in the cowl. Tiny Demons with bright, shining black eyes twinkled at her.

"**Pain**. And I don't want so much pain meds I get groggy and 'out-if-it.' I want to participate in my death.

Unconsciousness. Unable to communicate. Like when I really need something and am not able to say what it is. Being unconscious is when I lose all control, including my bowels and bladder."

The tiny group shivered in horror. All except Tiny Death, who merely shrugged. Fear, pain, unconsciousness, all that wasn't new to it.

Hadley continued: "**Procrastination!** I can't think of one word that means 'waiting a heck of a long time,' but this will do, because it means I'm afraid you won't show up when I want you and need you."

She closed her eyes.

She sighed.

She would Google for a synonym for "waiting a long time" in the morning. Right now, 'Procrastination' would have to do. She remembered a friend who died over a period of intense weeks in the hospital. When her grandson spoke at her funeral, he said, "Grandma's dying was borderline procrastination."

It was a good word.

"**Away.**" She said. "Away is such a big word with us old people. We're one fall away...we're just a stroke away...a memory away...and we all know the **away** is a bad place to be."

She frowned.

"I may be just hours away from dying, for all I know. Then again, I may live for years. I come from a line of strong women."

Hadley thought about the women in her family and how they knew all about death. Her great, great grandmother had sat in a cold Boston tavern and wrapped bandages during the Revolutionary War. Her pioneer ancestors had grabbed cast iron skillets and chased Death out of soddies where snakes dropped down through the earthen ceilings. And her grandmother sat for days beside her grandfather's deathbed and when, finally, Death, all in white this time, stood at the foot of the bed, Grandma looked up and whispered, "Where you been? Don't ya know we've been waitin' for ya?"

The little demons, after being named, were starting to fade, but Tiny Death stood strong and ready. Then it suddenly moved with the speed of light and sat down on her other knee. It seemed very confident and comfortable, tiny knees making the black robe stick up in front of it. "And that's not all!" She said it in a somewhat angry voice. Death didn't seem to mind.

The storm outside was growing bolder and Death seemed to notice it for the first time. Hadley glanced out the window as a blast of blizzard wind rattled the glass.

"**Terror.** What if I have one of those horrible, horrible diseases that rob you of every part of your humanness. Can I kill myself? That may be the last little bit of control I have left, and I may not be strong enough to do that."

Tiny Death looked bored. They had gone over that earlier.

A long-time friend and Hadley had once made a bond that if one of them asked the other to kill her, or at least help her die, she would. Trouble was – they couldn't figure out how to do it so the one doing the favor of the killing didn't get caught.

Details can be such a bitch.

For that matter, as they say, "Life's a bitch and then you die."

The tall lady in the soft robe continued naming the still-fading demons. Very little was left of them now.

"Fear of the **unknown**, although that isn't a biggie. Some days I get so tired a permanent sleep sounds like a good idea."

It seemed as if Hadley had finished the naming of her demons that surrounded her image of Tiny Death. They were gone from her knee.

"And you know what?" Tiny Death paid close attention. "Some people. When you mention death, say, 'Well, it's better than the alternative.' Wrong!" The little black-clothed figure seemed to jump a little at the strength of her voice. **Wrong!** bounced up against the wall. "Sometimes Death is the bringer of mercy and bearer of kindness."

Hadley and Death both nodded at that statement. Death actually must be a procrastinator. She heard so many people say, "It was time," after someone died. She took a breath.

She wasn't finished yet.

"I heard that a Pope said, 'Oh, God. I do not fear death, it is the dying.' Did you know my Aunt Ada firmly believed the streets of Heaven were paved with gold, not knowing that idea came from the last hopes of people who were dirt poor? Heaven was thought to be above, and Hell, if you believed in that, too, was below in the center of a boiling Earth. That was when people thought the earth was flat, so Heaven must be in the sky and Hell below ground."

Those flat Earth theories are still around.

Hadley shook her head. "Did you know the idea of Hell was plagiarized from the pagan religions and brought into Christianity to intimidate people into behaving?"

Tiny Death seemed to be very receptive to Theology lessons, although Hadley thought she could detect a small yawn under the cowl.

She sat quietly for a few minutes.

A different dimension made sense.

Energy was energy and could not be destroyed. She had seen Wes Longbow's spirit once, shortly after he died, for just a nano-second. Just standing before her, smiling. She had also seen an angel once.

No, it wasn't Death that scared her.

She held out her hand and the little figure hopped onto it. The wee skeletal feet were solid on Hadley's palm.

"You little Turkey," she smiled. "You follow old people around like a shadow that is there but not seen. Like smoke. Well, I don't have the guts or the knowledge so I can't very well kill myself. I'll have to trust you." Tiny Death seemed to smile inside the cowl.

"Remember that time Robbie had a really strong heart medicine and when we picked it up, I asked my good friend, who was the pharmacist, how many of those pills it would take to kill yourself. Remember how he smiled and said, 'You don't need those. Take 30 of these with a good bottle of wine and in three days your liver will collapse, and you'll die.' Remember how he held up a common over-the-counter pain killer? The bottle of wine didn't sound so bad. But I'd get a really expensive champagne."

She smiled and she was pretty sure Death smiled back, still standing firmly on her hand.

"You're Death. You're supposed to help us die. Can't hang myself. Don't know the knots Gun – don't have one. Knife – get a life! Although I do know to cut my arms up from wrist to elbow, not just slice across the wrists. Too chicken for that, and I don't have a car to put in a garage and leave running." Strangely enough, Hadley was sure Death yawned this time.

The husband of a friend had gotten a fatal diagnosis, come home, crawled into bed and refused to eat or drink. It took him only three weeks to die.

Hadley smiled. "All someone would have to do if I stopped eating or drinking, is bring some chocolate-frosted brownies and a good Chardonnay and I'd be sunk. Oh, and there was that story Rachael Steinberger told about her husband's mother who was living with them and Mama announced she wasn't eating any more. She was going to her room and stay there until she died. So, she disappeared into her room for three days and at the end of three days, she showed up at the dinner table again. 'Mama,' Rachael's husband said, 'I thought you were going to stop eating until you died.' And Mama looked at him like he was the dumbest person on earth and aid, 'Who wants to die on an empty stomach?'"

"Speaking of sweet stuff," she said.

She stood up and Tiny Death shot back into his picture frame and took up his place beside the brush. "Maybe I could choke to death on gummy bears and people could say I was killed by bears and just leave it at that."

She slipped into the kitchen and stole two chocolate chip cookies from her glass cookie jar. She looked at the cookies. "As Woody Allen said, 'I'm not afraid of dying. I just don't want to be there when it happens.'"

Marge had once said, "I like it when my doctor says something is normal for my age."

"Right," Hadley had responded. "And dying is normal for our age."

They had laughed and it was a good thing to laugh at Death.

"Oh God," she prayed out the window. "As I lay dying have people come by and tell me jokes!"

She didn't notice how the wind had become a roaring gale now. Drifts were piling up against the walls.

She looked one more time at the picture of "A Brush with Death," and smiled. More people should talk to Death, she thought. She patted the brush on its little top and straightened the little black cowl on Tiny Death. "I know how I'll meet you," she said to Death. "With what I used to say all the time:

Grace. Humor. Courage and Confidence."

Death didn't answer, but the wind suddenly died down and a gentle wisp of snow kissed the window.

REFLECTIONS FROM MARGE

Black bodies
swarm in
squeezed; shoved
locked
up.

The built bodies behind the metal bars
costs more than thousands of gold and silver.
Priceless, because it's free labor.

Mass incarceration of black men
Picked out from the street
funneled
at the mercy of the courts' feet.
A replay
of slavery days
with the first ship of African slaves---

Black bodies
swarm in
squeezed; shoved
locked
up.
The built bodies within the ships
costs more than a thousand words from the lips.
Priceless, because it was a free trip.

There are more black prisoners right now
than there were slaves in 1850!
The War on Drugs
was a war against black bodies!
Privatized to be the continuation of slavery.

1. www.powerpoems.com. *Corporate crime is the least punished crime in America.*

Marge

"I will feel guilty for the rest of my life."

"You didn't mean to do it."

"No, but I did it. I killed him."

"To feel guilty, you have to have done it on purpose. You did it to scare him. To feel guilty, you have to have had 'malice aforethought,' that's the law."

"I had lots of malice aforethoughts about shootin' Pickaxe for years!"

"When you shot him, you thought you were aiming above his head."

"I would have been if he hadn't been wearin' boots with heels and lifts! If he's painted his face he could have been Kiss, that weird music group. Short men!"

It was well into the wee hours of the morning. The blizzard outside was pounding against Marge's windows on the west side of Meadow Lakes Retirement Community like a covetous vampire insisting on being let in.

Marge and her cousin, Buckshot Betsy Bushwhacker sat in Marge's two comfortable living room chairs and watched the raging storm. They had talked for hours catching up. It had been good.

Now Marge was going deep into thought.

She was totally quiet.

"Atticus Finch," Marge said.

"I know that one," Betsy replied. *"To Kill A Mockingbird,"*

"That is a sin in the South," Marge added. "to kill a Mockingbird."

"Should be."

"In that book, everyone in town knows Tom Robinson did not rape and beat the white girl – everyone! Yet Tom is convicted. That book came out in 1960, but it's still true today. Our criminal justice system sucks. Betsy, you got off because people in Gospel Bird knew you and you were white. What if you had been a black or brown girl?"

Betsy shrugged. "And Raven was a super attorney."

Marge went back into her thoughts.

"I spent a lot of time on the street. And it's not just young black men, although there are more in prison now than were enslaved in 1850. It's youth, and even juveniles and in some schools, children as young as seven – SEVEN – have been arrested!"

When Marge is pissed, Marge is pissed.

"Most of the cops I worked with were good people, heroes even. There were a couple though, who thought the cops who shot blacks and browns and even white youth who ran, were the heroes."

She thought some more.

"Just Mercy," she said.

"That's a movie! I saw that!" Buckshot replied, looking at her cousin.

"It's the modern-day Atticus Finch story – a true story. This young defense attorney from Harvard

Law goes to Alabama, works for prisoners on death row."

"There ain't many on death row that can afford any attorney at all," Buckshot said.

Marge nodded.

"He finds all the evidence that Johnny D wasn't even near where a white woman was murdered, but the prosecutor and sheriff wanted a win, so they got him convicted with false testimony."

"Jamie Foxx was Johnny D. And what's not to like about Jamie Foxx?" Buckshot put both hands over her heart.

"He gets a hearing for a new trial," Marge continued as if Buckshot hadn't spoken. "And damned if the judge, a good old white boy in cahoots with the sheriff, denies Johnny a new trial. Because he confessed. Convicted again even when the witness told how he'd been threatened and bullied into false testimony. Bad system!"

Marge paused then went in a different direction.

"Do you know that if a camera is put in an interrogation room – which is a crappy, tiny, uncomfortable place, and that camera is behind the police and films the suspect – well, when people see a suspect, nervous, sweating, sometimes crying but confessing, a large percentage of people watching say, 'Yep – guilty as hell. He confessed.'"

Buckshot was interested and was still thinking about Jamie Foxx.

"BUT!" Marge said loudly. "If that camera is *behind the suspect* and focused on the cops interrogating the man or woman, a large percentage of the people viewing it say, 'Nope. Forced confession. Bullied him into confessing.'"

"Perspective," Buckshot mumbled.

A blast of wind rocked Marge's windows again. Wet snow clung to the glass then slid down to drop off onto the ground. It was as if God was throwing snowballs in agreement.

"Be white and corrupt enough and know friends in high places, you can kill somebody and get pardoned by the president," Buckshot said. "The president even bragged he could kill somebody and get away with it."

"Now DNA is proving a number of prisoners on Death Row are innocent."

She glanced out the window.

"Quite a storm," she said.

It was quiet for a minute.

They stood up.

Marge hugged her. "Time for bed, Sweet Girl."

Outside the blizzard reached its peak.

The windows shook again, as if trying to reach Marge and Buckshot as they turned toward their bedrooms.

REFLECTIONS FROM MARY ROSE

They do bad things to children in Africa I'm told
They castrate their girls, you know.
And all over the world
Children die of abuse
No big deal
We aren't the only ones
Everybody does it
That makes it right
So what if we are the only country
That shoots our own children
Who sees them running from their schools
Some with hands over their heads
Cell phones ring
Parents stiffen in panic
Children hide
Shots ring out
Sirens wail
Everybody does it
Not to worry
We send them our thoughts and prayers
We make promises
And memorials with flowers and teddy bears
The gun manufacturers meet with officials
In private
Nothing is done but to dig the graves.

"So would ya believe I was in Ireland all these years?"

Mary Rose McGill-Vondra could not stop looking at her brother. She remembered how he had nearly beaten the life out of their father when the drunken old man tried to rape her. They were in her bedroom. Teddy had dragged their father's unconscious body to the hallway, disappeared for a minute, then came back with his duffle bag over his shoulder.

His red sneakers were swinging from the handle.

For a time afterward, Mary Rose dreamed of those red sneakers, swinging a goodbye. That was all she saw in her dream.

Now here before her, after all these years, was a handsome man with a white beard and walking stick.

She couldn't believe how full of happiness she was.

Outside the blizzard was starting to move on, ready to attack Iowa.

"I was thinkin' about comin' back and findin' ya." Teddy spoke with the old Irish brogue that had been so familiar when they visited their father's grandparents. Soft. Inviting. Mary Rose had loved it and she found comfort in it now – again.

"I'd been a teacher," Teddy continued.

"Math," Mary Rose interrupted.

"Aye, Ya remember me well, girl."

There were two glasses of Bushmills Black Buch whiskey on the table between them.

The glasses were fine crystal, a wedding gift from Teddy.

The groom was sound asleep in the bedroom.
A gift from Wiley.

Mary Rose and Teddy had the night to themselves. "So, are ya comin' back I hope," Mary Rose said. She had picked up the brogue without ever thinking about it. It came naturally to both of them.

"Anon," Teddy said, shaking his head. "I was ready to come back to the states, and then something happened that made me sick to the quill."

He looked sad.

"I heard a long time ago about Columbine, the first shooting, and I thought how horrible that was, indeed."

Mary Rose perked up.

"Then time passed, and everyone just absorbed the horror and grief of it, let it be part of them, like a disease that goes dormant. And go dormant it did. It popped up again. Then it popped up again."

He looked at Mary Rose with a serious grimace. "How do ye stand it, girl? How can ya be in a society that shoots its own children while they're at their desks - - in a safe place - -for some of them a place even safer than their homes? How do ye stay in a place where the newest school equipment is an expensive, bullet-proof desk? A bullet-proof desk, when teachers have to pay for supplied outta their own pockets?" He shook his head.

They were quiet for a few minutes.

"I want to show you something," Mary Rose said. She reached for her cell phone.

"Search You Tube for Sandy Hook PSA," she told her phone, holding it in front of her lips.

"You're a right good techie, there, Sis," Teddy smiled.

Mary Rose didn't smile. She tapped the screen and handed the phone to her brother.

A boy, about middle school age, was running as fast as he could down a school hallway. "These sneakers my mom got are just what I need for the school year." He looks behind him at other children dashing down the hall.

A girl grabs a jacket and runs, "This jacket is a must have."

A girl is crouched on a toilet in a rest room stall. "I've got my own cell phone to say goodbye to my Mom."

We see she has typed in a text, "I love you Mom." Then there is silence until you hear it.

A man's footsteps on the bathroom floor. Step. Step. Step.

Blackness.

Both Mary Rose and Teddy have tears in their eyes.

"So, I can't stay here," Teddy says. Handing the phone back. "Some of the people who think this is the most wonderful place in the world don't recognize how much help ya need. You have more infant deaths than twenty-six other countries." He shook his head again. "Twenty-six. I read it on the plane comin' over."

"We have a lot of hungry kids, too," Mary Rose added. "The schools feed them."

"Aye. And ye tend to blame the victim here. A girl gets raped – her fault. A child gets sick – parents are bad. People are poor – shoulda worked harder."

"Ya know, the people who think they know it all, who think there's nothin' wrong here, they're the ones who say, 'Love it or Leave It'. Well, I left it, and America's lost more than one good teacher because of what's goin' on here."

Mary Rose leaned forward in her chair. "When we were young, I thought by the time we reached this age everything would be fixed. Everything would be all right and we would be taking care of each other."

"There's a lot of that, too, m'dear sister. Look at your friends, your new husband, how people here care for each other and how many of ye here volunteer at schools or churches or food lines for the homeless. There are good, good people everywhere. We just can't seem to get 'em all in one place."

"I know," Mary Rose admitted. "But when I heard we put babies in cages and are turning away Christian refugees at our border, I thought of Mary and Joseph, being refugees themselves with baby Jesus."

Teddy made the sign of the cross over his heart.

"And if Jesus appeared at the border now, he wouldn't be a white man with a gun. He'd be a brown man with a child on his back."

The blizzard had changed to a gentle, big-flake snow and Norman Rockwell was back again.

Teddy stood up. Mary Rose followed.

"I'm gettin' up early, Mary Rose. I may not see ye again. I'm glad I came this time and maybe, just maybe, if you and Wiley stay healthy, you can take a honeymoon in the old country and come visit me."

"You are the greatest wedding present in the world," Mary Rose said, and she broke into tears, laid her head on her brother's shoulder and sobbed.

"Aye," he said. "Every girl needs a good cry now and then."

Tears were running down his cheek and into her soft, dyed blonde hair.

As Teddy walked past the big window at the end of Mary Rose's hall on the way to his guest room, he could see a full moon shining brightly through the trees outside of Meadow Lakes Retirement Community. The unbroken snow glittered and sparkled.

"Aye," he said to himself, "the Cold Full Moon of December. A good time for a Norman Rockwell scene in life."

The light of the beautiful Cold Full Moon followed him down the hall.

A Note from Joy

When I told people this was, both in title and reality, *The Last BOOB Girl Book*, several ladies said, "Oh, you've said that before." No, I never did. I planned when I started BOOB Girls II, *Lies, Spies and Cinnamon Rolls* that I hoped to live long enough to write twelve books in honor of Table 12.

Twelve years later – twelve books.

A good friend said, "You can't stop. They mean too much to you."

Wrong again.

I have other things to write, even at age eighty-one, I have more dreams. I want to write, probably blogs, called *Four Pours*. I want to write about three other women with whom I want to share a good bottle of wine – women of the past and women of the present, four at a time, that means three and me. It will be fun, so to read those, go to www.theboobgirls.com and sign up to receive my emails.

But these beautiful BOOB Girls have slept with me, traveled with me, talked with me, showed up in unexpected places and led me to more people and more friends than I could ever hope for.

My husband, Ted, once said, "You have ten thousand friends, and you keep in touch with all of them!"

What a terrific compliment, and I count you as one of them.

I got letters from ladies who were seriously ill who said they read BOOB Girls I two or even three times because it was all that made them laugh. I autographed books for sisters and mothers who were on hospice. I called a quilting club as a surprise for a birthday girl fan, I spoke to the most wonderful institutions imaginable – the small-town library. I ended up having given well over five hundred BOOB Girl Talks. Each was filled with laughter and hugs.

I met a lady who read about Mary Rose McGill reinventing herself with a new wardrobe. She had decided she had so few years left she didn't need any new clothes. After Mary Rose and the adventures of the girls, she decided she had a lot of life left. She took her daughter and granddaughter shopping, got a new wardrobe, a new hairstyle and, like Mary Rose, red-rimmed glasses.

Her granddaughter became her fashion consultant. "Remember Grandma, when you wear your tight jeans, they go inside those boots." You go girl!

We had a *BOOB Girls Bold* article in my blog and urged all the BOOB Girls to do something brave, different and outlandish for one week. I wore a *Walking Dead* T-shirt every day. Lucy had a manicure with bright blue polish.

And the biggest thrill – my two surrogate grandsons adapted BOOB Girls I into a standing-room only musical with a fabulous cast, unbelievable music and cheering, standing ovations. Then, Sue Mouttet, who played Maggie Patten, read the book onto audio tape. The book – read by the REAL Maggie Patten.

And my computer cooperated most of the time, was managed by another surrogate grandson when it refused to do so, and I kept writing, my life went on. My beloved husband, Marv, died before he could read book five. By the time book eight came out, I had met Ted, my beloved husband now.

Through the sorrow and the tears, the laughter and the joy, and you – I think I am one of the luckiest women alive.

I realized about mid-way through the series, that we are ALL the BOOB Girls.

We have the feistiness and fierceness of Maggie Patten, the dignity of Hadley, the innocence of Mary Rose, the intelligence of Robbie and the street smarts of Marge Aaron.

All we need is a red cane.

Most of all, I want you to remember:
You are beautiful.
Just look at you!
Your face is sculpted by joy and sorrow,
tears and laughter.
Your hair is blown thin by winds of experience.
And there is so much knowledge and wisdom in
your head, your head can't hold it all.
It has to trickle down through the rest of your
body, and that's why you may have gotten a little
thicker as you aged.

Beyond that - you have Grace, Humor, Courage and Confidence.

You are a BOOB Girl and I thank you for being my friend.

The BOOB Girls Tour –
where they've been in all the books

It's fun to get a car full of friends and explore Omaha and where the girls have been. Some BOOB Girls from out of town make it a delightful overnight trip. If you do that, let us know. We'll meet you at Marks.

Two musts on the tour, if you've read **BOOB Girls XI, *The Gun found at Marks***, are **Marks Bistro** and the Durham Museum. Marks is the girls' favorite restaurant at 51st and Underwood Street. If the weather is nice, have lunch on the most beautiful patio in Omaha. May I suggest Mark's famous Mac and Cheese and ask for Mark. He'll be happy to say hello; show you Joy and Marv's table – which is also Marge and her husband's - and the table where Warren Buffett met with Hillary Clinton.

The Durham is at 810 South 10th Street and is in the historic old Union Station. The folks at the information center can direct you to the scale model of the Trans-Mississippi Exposition of 1898. While you are there, tour the museum and see the historic railroad cars and a lot of Omaha history.

End your visit with a hearty ice cream cone, Sundae or other treat at their old-fashioned ice cream counter.

Not far away is **Prospect Hill Cemetery,** where Anna Wilson and Dan Allen are buried. It is one of those best-kept secrets. Between 31st and 33rd Streets, bordered by Parker and Grant Streets. Each Memorial Day the cemetery hosts a reenactment featuring historic Omahans who are buried there and Anna Wilson's obituary is read at her grave. It's a delight and the location is historic and beautiful. Residents of early Omaha used to picnic there on Sundays. It's worth a visit.

So is **Forest Lawn** where the Joslyns and other Omaha dignitaries are buried. It's at 7909 Mormon Bridge Rd, and if you want to visit the Mormon Bridge, that's where Gertrude and Heathcliff Hosemoff from book V tried to die together by jumping into the river but landed in a cruise boat swimming pool instead.

Wolf Brothers Western Store, where Wiley went to buy a new western sport coat, was one of my late husband Marv's favorite places to shop. Located at 70th and Dodge, it's an old Omaha landmark with great stuff.

Metropolitan Community College (Metro) where Ken David David is going and where he met Denise, has several campuses, but the most beautiful is at 5300 North 30th Street and was actually the old Fort Omaha, built in 1868.

The Holland Center, where the gang went to hear the Omaha Symphony Pops concert, is at 13th and Douglas, an easy walk from the heart of the **Old Market**. The Holland is beautiful and has perfect acoustics. Two of my grandchildren have played there with the Omaha Area Youth Orchestra. A beautiful little restaurant is hidden inside.

Nope, I'm sorry; there is no **Salem's Crossing, Nebraska. Ben Schroeder**, another surrogate grandson, loves Highway 30 so I let him set its location. He located it just North of Wood River which is two and a half hours west of Omaha just off I-80. Head there and you can see everything the girls saw and if you drive far enough, there's the **Great Platte River Road Arch**, Sandhill Cranes, Grand Island and America the Beautiful with amber waves of grain.

The Arboretum on Farnam Drive at 8141 Farnam, where Ted and I live, and the retirement community upon which Meadow Lakes is modeled, is just east of Methodist Hospital..

The Bookworm, where the girls browsed after coffee at **The Grinder** has moved. Get back on 84th, drive south to Center Street, turn right to 90th, then right again and you're at the new location. Go in and check to see how their supply of BOOB Girls books is holding up. The Bookworm is one of the finest independent bookstores you'll ever enjoy.

There really is a **Finicky Frank's** restaurant in Omaha and it's excellent. It's just off I-680 at the 30th Street exit. Go north a very short way, turn left into a short road leading to the gas station and to Finicky's. My favorite thing there is the breaded pork loin.

If you are coming from West Omaha, go to 105th and Pacific, then turn south until you find the beautiful **Happy Hollow Country Club** where Hadley has taken the group in nearly every one of the early books. Unless it's lunch or dinner time, you can probably find Kelly or Jim to show you the library, the girls' favorite room. Dorothy, who had worked at "Happy" for many years, died a few years ago. The place will never be the same.

Drive on east to 72nd Street and turn left. Now you're at the area where **Morgan Graves** furnished La Viva Crypt from the Lazy Leopard Lounge auction and put everything in book IV, ***Murder at Meadow Lakes.***

Keep driving north to 72nd and Maple. Turn right to 6406 Maple and you'll be at **Centering Corporation**. This is the grief resource center Joy and Dr. Marvin Johnson founded in 1977. Come in and say hello. Inside is Caring Cups Coffee Stop.

You'll leave Centering, turn left and drive up Maple Street. Drive through the little village and you'll see where once was Jane's Health Market and up the street is Leo's Diner, along with Centering Corporation, they are all in the village of **Benson.**

Continue on to 49th Street and turn right. Keep driving and you'll be at the **Homy In**n where the girls went for champagne on tap. As you drive across Happy Hollow, look to your right. At the end of the block, by what is lovingly called the traffic peanut, is Dan Simpson's Auto Shop. Danny found the hidden tracker in the Hummer in ***BOOB Girls V.***

Head south until you come to West Center Street. Turn left on Center and drive by **Kubat**

Pharmacy, one of the few remaining family-owned pharmacies and where the girls bought the bedpan for Mary Rose's bedpan hat in *BOOB Girls II.*

Continue east on Center Street and you'll come to the **Old Market.** Now you're on your own. Visit **Wheatfield's, The Jackson Street Tavern, M's** and of course, **Ted and Wally's Ice Cream**. Stand beside the new Hyatt Place Hotel and look up at the third floor of the Mayfair Building across 12th Street. The apartment near the back by the fire escape was Joy and Marv's and Robbie's. You'll be standing where Esmeralda sang her sad song to Robbie, then patted the beautiful horse in *BOOB Girls III.* Go into the **Passageway Mall** where Wes and Hadley had dinner and go smell the leather at Overland Sheepskin where Wes bought a jacket. Keep walking east and you'll come to the former **ConAgra** campus and lake.

If it's a nice day and you want to walk even more, the **Bob Kerrey Pedestrian Bridge** across the wide Missouri is just a little way north.

Now drive back on Center Street to 84th Street. Turn left on 84th and go to **Mangelsen's**, where you can find just about everything you need, including help making a bedpan hat.

Go south to Interstate 80 by Mangelsen's and head west. Drive to the Springfield exit and head south to Louisville. There you'll visit **Coop de Ville** on Main Street, the neatest little gift shop ever. Walk around the corner to the big white house and explore **Feathers,** the other gift shop decorated by Dr. Liz and her ladies. Have one of Dr. Liz's Scotcheroos and, like Robbie – buy a purse. It's sayings from the Coop bathroom that start the fifth book when Mary Rose looks in the mirror. "I do declare, I love my hair." That bathroom is worth a trip to Louisville anytime.

Get back on the highway by Louisville and drive a short distance to the sign reading South Bend. It's on State Highway 66. If it's close to dinner time, head for **Round the Bend Steakhouse**, home of the Testicle Festival. Careful. Don't miss it, it's on your left and high on a hill. The Ragged Ass Saloon in the first book is modeled after Round the Bend.

After too much food at the Bend, go north until you get to I-80 again. Head west to exit 420. There is **Pine Grove RV Resort**, former home of Marv and Joy and where the girls went on their Staycation in book V.

Come in! Have a cup of coffee. Be sure to register at the office. Go on to **Baker's Candies** in Greenwood and shop, shop, shop at the factory store. The gift shop is chocolate heaven.

You can dedicate an entire day to the **Henry Doorly Zoo,** where Marge and Alphonso had a date.

I'm sorry, but there is no **Peyton's Hair Salon**. I picture it in one of the big apartment buildings near the river in the Old Market.

I imagine I've left out some places. But if you want to follow the girls to Gospel Bird, Alaska, I'll be happy to direct you there.

Enjoy! And thank you for being part of Table 12.

About the Author

Joy Johnson (Brown) is 80+ years old now! With her late husband, Dr. Marvin Johnson, she founded Centering Corporation (www.centering.org), North America's oldest and largest Bereavement Resource Center, and Grief's Journey, a Center for Grieving Children in Omaha, Nebraska. She has written or edited over 100 books on grief, many for children. After she retired from Centering Corporation in 2009, she began writing The *BOOB Girls: The Burned Out Old Broads at Table 12.* There are now eleven books in the series.

Joy has three children and six grandchildren. Her marriage to Ted brought another son, daughter-in-law and granddaughter into her family. During book ten, Joy and Ted were full-time RVers, traveling to Alaska and the West Coast. Now they are home once again in the Arboretum, a retirement community in Omaha, the city where most of their children live. Joy does over thirty BOOB Girls presentations annually, with Ted as her wheelman and manager – and sex object as well.

Visit the girls and Joy Johnson at:

www.theboobgirls.com

https://www.theboobgirls.com/blog

Like us on Facebook:
https://www.facebook.com/TheBoobGirls/

Bring Some Joy to Your Group

Joy Johnson Brown speaks to over fifty groups each year with a humorous presentation on The Making of A BOOB Girl. Contact her for your state, national or local conference or meeting at joy.johnson@msn.com or through her website at www.theboobgirls.com.

To speak to her by phone call 1-402-639-2939

Email: joy.johnson@msn.com

If you enjoy this book, you'll love and laugh with:

The Boob Girls: The Burned Out Broads at Table 12
The Boob Girls II: Lies, Spies and Cinnamon Roles
The Boob Girls III: Sandhills and Shadows
The Boob Girls IV: Murder at Meadow Lakes
The Boob Girls V: The Secret of the Red Cane
The Boob Girls VI: From the Eye of the Moose
The Boob Girls VII: Ten Little Puritans
The Boob Girls VIII: Learning to Love Willie
The Boob Girls IX: The Boob Girls in Training Bras
The Boob Girls: X: The Gospel Bird
The Boob Girls XI: The Gun Found at Marks
The Boob Girls XII: The Last BOOB Girl Book!

 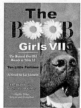   

Buy the set for $150.00, includes *The BOOB Girls I* Audio CD, **www.theboobgirls.com**

331